To Nigel

WHITE SAND

By Simon Kerr

Read it, and weep.

29/10/14

First Published 2014 by BLACK FLAG.

A CIP Catalogue record for this book
is available from the British Library

ISBN: 978-0-9930324-0-0

This novel is dedicated to the Disappeared,
and the families of those people killed and disappeared,
by all parties to the conflict in Northern Ireland.
May they all find closure and peace someday soon.

Name (date of disappearance)	Organisation Responsible	Date recovered/Still missing
Jean McConville (1972)	I.R.A.	corpse recovered August 2003
Seamus Wright (1972)	I.R.A.	still missing
Kevin McKee (1972)	I.R.A.	still missing
Joseph Lynskey (1972)	I.R.A.	still missing
Peter Wilson (1973)	I.R.A.	corpse recovered November 2010
Eamon Molloy (1975)	I.R.A.	corpse recovered 1999
Columba McVeigh (1975)	I.R.A.	still missing
Hugh McVeigh (1975)	U.D.A.	corpse recovered September 1975
David Douglas (1975)	U.D.A.	corpse recovered September 1975
Samuel Miller (1976)	U.D.A.	corpse recovered September 1977
Robert Nairac (1977)	I.R.A.	still missing
Brendan Megraw (1978)	I.R.A.	still missing
John McClory (1978)	I.R.A.	corpse recovered June 1999
Brian McKinney (1978)	I.R.A.	corpse recovered June 1999
Gerard Evans (1979)	I.R.A.	corpse recovered October 2010
Danny McIlhone (1981)	I.R.A.	corpse recovered November 2008
Charlie Armstrong (1981)	I.R.A.	corpse recovered July 2010
Eugene Simmons (1981)	I.R.A.	corpse recovered May 1984
James Galway (1982)	U.V.F.	corpse recovered November 1983
Seamus Ruddy (1985)	I.N.L.A.	still missing
Brian O'Raw (1997)	U.V.F.	corpse recovered September 1997
Gareth O'Connor (2003)	I.R.A.	corpse recovered 2005
Lisa Dorrian (2005)	U.V.F.	still missing

Mother missing a month

Belfast News Reporter. (17th January 1973)

A widow and mother of five children, rumoured to have been taken from her Donard Flats home by the I.R.A. over a month ago has not been seen or heard from since.

Mrs. Mary McCandless (39), of 42 Donard Flats, was at home with her family last December 7th at 7.30pm when, according to her daughter Natalie, over ten I.R.A men and women broke into the flat and took her away.

Mrs. McCandless has not been seen since and her children and their 70-year-old grand-mother, who lives nearby, have not reported the matter to the police for a month.

The children are aged between three and nineteen. Three of the older children are not at home. Ruth, nineteen, is in hospital. Martin, seventeen, is interned in Long Kesh. Fifteen-year-old Natalie, is looking after her two younger brothers, Eddie, aged five, and Frankie aged thirteen, living on an Army widow's pension.

The family have been resident in the Flats since they were forced to flee their home in East Belfast during the '69 Troubles.

Hero Father Dead

Their father Harold, who won the D.S.M. with the 'Chindits' in W.W.2, died last year of lung cancer and the family moved recently from one section of the Flats to their present address at No 42.

Natalie said that the night before being taken away her mother had lured out of a bingo session by a young woman who claimed one of her children had been injured.

"My mother was hooded, badly beaten, robbed of her purse, handbag, shoes and coat. She was found wandering the streets by soldiers of the Scots Guard.

"That was all my mother could tell me about the incident, and then the following night she was taken again," Natalie said.

The children were afraid to report the incident to the police or the Army. They hoped their mother would be returned by now.

PART ONE

1

"What did you tell the Brits?"

There was no answer because she was deep in shock, throat salt-dry and there was no breath left to make the words. Her animation came in short crackles, rasps of hot air in and out so quickly as to be useless to her lungs. The Spar bag—she could make out that familiar green tree logo... The Spar bag they'd dragged over her clotted head was suffocating her. The oxygen in the hotter and hotter air, in her shrinking world of tears, blood and sweat getting less, and less.

"Tell us, you whore you."

She was struck again, could not see the fist coming, stiffening, in the face again, red lightning flared from her jaw under her left ear. The blow knocked it into her, rocked the chair beneath her, the realisation:

I'm going to die—like this.

2

It was the night of the seventh of December. Elsewhere in West Belfast her children were home alone, terrified, wondering when she was coming back to take care of them.

She'd been in the bath when the Provos smashed their way in. It was her one indulgence. A hot bath on a Wednesday night, a relaxing soak.

She locked the bathroom door, turned the bare bulb off, lit a candle, and undressed in sputtering privacy. The kids knew well enough not to disturb her. "There's something wrong with her head again isn't there?" she'd overheard Frankie say to Natalie before tea.

She dipped her foot into the steaming water—so hot it nearly burnt the toes off her, but she liked it that hot for shaving her legs. Her husband Harold always said she'd scald herself one day and he'd have to piggy back her up to the Royal's Casualty because there was no other way to get her there in time to save her.

She plonked her other foot in, and then knelt down in the water. The heat-surge of immersion, the water roiling up round her bum, was nearly maddening, but it passed, like all feelings passed. Like the pain from the previous night's interrogation would pass?

She scooped hot water up and ladled it onto her bruised breasts, catching her flickering shadow doing the same thing

11

on the wall behind, tending to the injuries inflicted by a phantom baton.

Why do people do such terrible things to each other?

She looked to the candle, as if at Mass, in the church, as if expecting an answer to this—

Why do this to me? I never hurt anyone. Or at least, I try not to.

Watching the candle-flame lick around the wick: in the silence only a faint hissing.

With a sigh she gripped the sides of the bath, pushed up, straightened her legs and slid down into the soothing soaking water until, until her little body was under, and only her battered face broke the surface. Harold envied the fact she could lie back in the bath, submerge 'like a wee porpoise': he'd been a big man, a big fighting man, but in the bath he was all knees and elbows.

Two of her children had been conceived in baths—after the water had cooled down. She closed her eyes as she, his wee porpoise, went under.

The front door of Flat 42 gave way after two sledgehammer hits to the lock. Eight armed and masked men charged into the maisonette, flanked by four women, only three of whom wore masks.

"I.R.A.," the leading man yelled to make it officially a Provisional action.

The kids inside started screaming; Frankie, the eldest boy at thirteen, fiercest: 'Mum.'

They were all told to 'Shut the fuck up!" at gunpoint. And ordered to "Get out of the way!" as the men smashed through the flat looking for the radio transmitter they had been ordered to, but were not to find.

It was the unmasked woman, a bleach-blonde with beady blue eyes, who kicked the bathroom door in, smoked out the candle, and set about fishing her out of her underwater sanctuary. She was dragged up into the air by the hair, just in time, whoosh of water leaving her ears, to hear the pronouncement:

"Mary McCandless. You're under the arrest of the People's Army."

There was this terrible long-no-movement-moment of shock, then, she heard wee Eddie crying out 'Mum!' It was only then she began to struggle, to claw at the woman's hands, to scream: "Leave my kids alone, you bitch."

The unmasked blonde beat her down with hard bony fists, trying to subdue her.

Her elbow cracked into the side of the bath, but she didn't give up. "Frankie?" she cried, "Eddie? Are you all right?"

Masked men came in and dragged her shrieking-naked out of the bath, into the hall, and out the smashed front door, into the open.

Fight: She lashed out at the men, tried to rip off one's balaclava, but something hit her hard in the nose, stunned her—legs buckling—and she fell to the ground.

Gloved hands pinned her there, laid out on the concrete.

She heard the squealing of Eddie, getting round the Provos, and to her: "Mummy. Mummy."

And Frankie: "Get off her you bastards."

Wee Eddie curled around her. "Let her go, leave her alone," he cried, clinging on to her naked arms, breasts, anything his tiny hands could grab onto, for dearest life.

Hands reached down, trying to peel him off her. *No—they would not drag Eddie away, not while there was a breath in her chest.* She kicked against the force holding her legs, trying to break free, strike out, but it was no good.

"Calm down," she was told by the bleach blonde, who

was holding her hands down, "No one will hurt the kids if you calm down and come quietly."

Dazed and weak and weeping, but still full of that mothering instinct to protect, she let the *Cumann na mBan* women pick Eddie off her. They got her to her feet and pulled an old summer dress of hers over her wet-slick head and onto her soaking skin—it was the one patterned with red roses that she'd worn when Harold had taken her on the train to Bangor for May Day.

Frankie tried to break through the throng of masked men to try to help her. Handgun-to-hothead, he was told to: "Back off kid or be shot."

"This a mistake,' Frankie yelled back, "A mistake." He could not understand why the Provos, his heroes, would do such a thing.

"It's all right," she called to her son. "It's all right. Look after the others for me."

They pushed her away from her kids, and she let them, taking the danger away with her. They walked her barefoot, down cold concrete pavements and out of the labyrinth of the Donard Flats Complex.

"Where are you taking me?" she asked the blonde without the mask.

"For a wee chat," came the blonde's reply, followed by a phlegm-rattling chuckle. "You know the drill."

"My kids need someone to look after them."

"You'll be back in no time if you cooperate. Now come on."

Frankie followed her, disobeying—at a distance. Despite repeated warnings from the Provos that he would be kneecapped, *they wouldn't shoot a kid*, he kept coming, her boy her hero, the son of her Chindit hero, his father's son...

Right up to the point where they bundled her into the side
-door of a hijacked green V.W. Camper van. Right up to the
point they pulled the bag over her head. She didn't know,
couldn't see, what happened after that. She was taken away.

3

"Tell us or we'll kill you," her interrogator shouted as loud as he could, going hoarse, "I fucking mean it."

The quickening of the breath, the gasping, the frenzied struggle against the ropes, that was now somehow over. The cramps in her feet, the tingling, buzzing bees in her hands, had passed. Inside the plastic bag, she was dizzy, less and less present, even more detached from things, floating away: *There. They said it—finally admitted as much. They're going to kill me.*

And it was almost a relief to hear those words. Part of her, the lover whose life had been his, had so wanted to not be there, to stop, since he had passed away last January... And yet, the mother in her had to live on for the kids—the eldest would cope, but Eddie was still so young—for him if nothing else.

How can they kill a woman—a mother like their own?

People who knew the I.R.A.'s code of conduct would tell you, if a local unit tried and judged you'd committed a crime against 'the Movement', as a woman, you could expect a good hiding. You could maybe expect to get your head shaved. You might even expect to get tarred and feathered. The most punishment you could expect was to be told to leave the area and never come back, or else. You would not expect to done in like a dog in some derelict safe house somewhere.

They're going to kill me like a dog. Like they killed Provo and Stickie.

Provo and Stickie were Frankie's two rescue mongrels,

jokingly named after the two factions of the I.R.A.: the young Provisionals, who were all for all-out war since '69, and the older Official faction, who'd declared a ceasefire on May twenty-ninth that year, 1972.

Harold's party-piece of a night-in with friends—using Stickie as a ventriloquist's dummy, opening and closing his fanged mouth, sending up the Marxist Chief of Staff, Goulding: "We're sticking to our ceasefire. We're committed to 'Stages': achieving a United Ireland by defensive measures and political agitation alone. We simply cannot win with the limited tactics of abstention and physical force…"

People, *their neighbours? their neighbours kids?* who knew rumours of them and little else, lured Frankie's warring dogs up the towers, no doubt with some scraps of meat, then picked them up—they were trusting little souls, opened the hatch of the multi-storey rubbish chute, and shoved them in.

The fall killed them dead.

It was three days of searching high and low before Frankie, gutted, found their bloating remains in the garbage. (Frankly, he blamed his Mum for this. If she hadn't prayed over that wounded Brit soldier it wouldn't have happened.)

4

Why do you think you're here? What crime have you committed? If you were innocent you wouldn't be here!

If she had not done what they accusing her of, been a tout, what did she do that was so wrong? What was her crime truly, what could she admit to, confess? What deserved a death sentence?

Thinking, *Being born a Protestant?*

Her birthday, 25ᵗʰ August 1933, would then be the date of her crime.

But there's nothing wrong with being born, is there? Her mind, even starved of air, blood ringing in her ears, could not accept that explanation. That was ridiculous.

Then, was the offence more complicated than mere delivery into the world?—more correctly her being conceived as a Protestant at 113 Oates Road, in East Belfast. The product of two adult humans' comfort seeking—the laborious male, Brian Smith, the tired-out female, June, engaged in a late night coupling, neither of whom really experienced orgasm as such but nevertheless, there was the gloopy warmth of an ejaculation, an end, and enough relief to get to sleep.

Thinking, *Was this then my sin?* The Original Sin. The beginning of life. God help her, she would not accept that.

Thinking, *Being brought up a Prod?*

It might have been a crime if she had grown up to let the bigotry and intolerance of the time blind her, narrow her mind, but her upbringing in the shadow of Goliath and Samson, the mighty yellow cranes at the Harland & Wolff shipyard, had not stopped her falling in love at first sight with a Roman Catholic. Had not stopped her loving Harold more each day they worked together as domestic servants in the Watson household on the Hollywood Road. Had not stopped her marrying him in 1952, at the tender age of nineteen—with her parents' reluctant consent, many congratulations to the happy couple.

Thinking, *Was it because Harold had served in the British Army in World War Two and continued to serve in overseas tours of duty up until 1964?*

No. That wasn't a crime: the Army had nothing to do with her and she wanted nothing more to do with the army that took Harold away from her so many times. The heartache, the rows, accusations of nagging.

Thinking, *Was it her mixed marriage?*

Maybe, but then, she converted?

Was it my conversion, then?

Surely though, changing her religion to make things simpler for Harold, and rearing the children, had been the best thing she could do?

She'd attended Clonard Monastery religiously for Catholic instruction from 1964 on. A lost sheep in this new flock, she did everything they asked of her. Sent her kids to St. Malaghey's primary school across the town, on the Antrim Road, in spite of the consequences.

Was it because I was dubbed 'a turncoat', a 'Judas'?

Both sides of the widening divide seemed to disapprove of her actions, to see her as someone who didn't belong to either camp, Orange or Green, but what more could she have done to show her sincerity to those who mattered to her?

Love Harold.

Honour Harold.

Obey Harold, mostly.

Till death do us part.

These were the vows she had taken in the sight of God, the white mist of her veil lifted, and she had not taken them lightly.

Till death do us part, do us part: *Was it the fact that my lover and protector had died—because I was a widow, alone and defenceless?*

People were supposed to look after widows and orphans—for the Bible tells them so.

A single mother?

Did the fact that Social Security payments and her Army widow's pension were so miserable mean that she was gagging to take bribes from the security forces to spy on I.R.A. movements around the Falls—the same security forces who had interned her Martin the day he turned seventeen— honestly?

Or was it because of those sleeping pills…

Being a bad mother, such a bad mother, so selfish to want to join Harold in heaven, so bad?

Those pills, tranquillisations lined up on the dining table: four rows of seven blue barbiturate dots. No one else around.

(That familiar vision in her mind of her children standing around a hospital death-bed finally understanding how hard it had been for her on her own, how unfair it had been of people to make her an outcast, how much heartache, the anguish she had endured.)

Yes. Being a no-good mother, she would admit it, had never denied it to anyone other than Brigid, her mother-in-law—that was surely a crime that called for punishment, for the purifying wrath of the Lord her shepherd, in this place of torment, her valley of the shadow of, was this life?

*

Her crime against the Movement, or rather her offence, was to kneel down under fire, and to cradle a young British soldier in her arms, saying the Lord's Prayer with him: *Our Father who art in Heaven, hallowed be thy name, thy kingdom come, thy will be done on Earth as it is in Heaven…* The boy, he was only a skinny eighteen, seemed to be bleeding from a wound in his chest. He had been cut off from his unit in the mayhem of a gun battle and shot at by an I.R.A. sniper—and this outside her flat. "Please help me. Please. I don't want to die." He was banging on her front door. "I don't want to die. Somebody…"

She and the kids regularly took cover, lying down, when the gunfire started.

The firing went on, *crack! crack!* Ricochet whines. "Help"—a weak gasp heard in a brief lull.

The thought that this could have been Harold, lying dying in Burma or wherever, begging not to be alone, not just another anonymous man in uniform needing, bleeding, made her get up and go to the door.

"Are you mad Mum?"—shouted Frankie—"Catch yourself on!" She opened it.

"Stay there," she told her kids, and she helped him.

When their prayers were over, and the firing had ceased, his comrades and the medics came and took him away on a stretcher. The prayers were answered, her prayers: he was still alive.

For this, the morning after, they painted BRIT LOVER all over the door in red paint. For this, they stoned all of the windows of the flat in the following evening. For this, giving comfort to the enemy, they would do so much more.

She walked back into the house, covered in blood, and closed the door. The first to accuse her, Frankie shouted at her: "What are you doing helping those bastards?"

She slapped her own son across the face for saying that. "He was somebody's boy. Some day maybe you'll understand that."

He was Harold, for her, for a moment.

A bloody mark on Frankie's cheek, fury in his eyes.

She went to wash the blood off her hands. It had coagulated and was hard to scrub off, but she managed. As the pinked water flowed down the plughole, she caught her reflection in the bathroom mirror—she saw somebody there she almost didn't recognise, *the Good Samaritan, the Good Samaritan,* the Mary she had been when she was with Harold, a woman who did not fear the pain of life, anymore than she feared death.

(Some newspaper accounts claimed the unknown soldier died in Mary's arms but not a word of a lie, he lived on, even if he has never been traced.)

5

Natalie would have been coming home with the fish and chips. Because the oven in the new flat had not been connected, Natalie would have been coming home. And all their neighbours from the Flats, they'd all have been out gossiping. Pointing. Laughing. Jeering. After. Poor Natalie would have known then that something terrible had happened, something else. And she'd have come running at breakneck speed, regretting that ciggy she'd had with the others on the street corner before she'd gone into Kearney's Chippy.

"Hurry back. Don't stop for a sneaky smoke either," she'd told Natalie, the rock of the family, the one she'd come to rely on through the depression, through the breakdowns, the suicide attempt, hospitalisations, the E.C.T. therapy; the one she'd tried to make hard enough to take it, life, at fourteen, because at thirty-nine she wasn't anymore.

Were these going to be her last words to the bravest little girl in the whole wide world—this girl who'd saved her life…

About a bloody cigarette!

*

Virgo, for the month of December: over a strong cup of tea, Natalie had tried to cheer her up by reading the *Good Housekeeping* horoscope to her that very afternoon.

That bleakness, that darkness, written all over her face. She could feel it there, the lack, the black nothing. She was thinking about how when she went like this, lost, that only Harold knew what to do, that what Natalie was doing was futile.

The rules of the game are changing. It's time to put yourself first. Overcome your hesitancy, use that quiet determination and reach out for your goal. You are more capable than you dreamed; it's just a question of adjusting your attitude.

Virgo the virgin. *How could a mother of five still be Virgo?*

She looked at Natalie. Natalie could be a Virgo. That is, if Natalie had not been an Aries? The ram. If Natalie had not let any of the horny local lads at her?—No. The look on Natalie's face, the innocence of youth, that unsullied glow of hope, testified that her Natalie was still a good girl.

"Don't you think this means we should leave here Mum?" Natalie said, naively, trying to get her to open up.

Leave?

It's just a question of adjusting your attitude.

But to lose yet another home—after just moving into it? Become refugees without shelter for the fifth time in two years? At the mercy of the gunmen? Constantly intimidated by the threat of Loyalist attacks. Harassed by the Brits, these seventeen-year-old squaddies, who were serving Her Majesty, enforcing Direct Rule, restoring law and order with Self-Loading Rifles. Her kids in the streets, dodging sniper bullets and covering fire?

"We can't leave darling. There's nowhere else to go." Her

voice sounded funny—why?—it was the first time she'd spoken since she'd woken up.

Natalie grabbed a hold of her hand, trying to maintain contact. "Tell me what happened Mum, please. Talk to me. I know you're upset but…"

But, there it was again.

The black lack.

In the early days, when Harold was home from his soldiering on, he tried to make her happy with jokes, silly Sinatra singing *Mack the Wife*; later on it was dancing with the doomed dogs and teasing the doomed kids; later still telling her to pull herself together woman; finally he learnt to just wait. That it was futile. The struggling against it. Reality. All efforts futile. In times dark. She would find her way back to him eventually. He was her love, the love of her life. Waiting for her.

"Tell me Mum?" Natalie pressed her knuckles white. "Tell me what they asked you about?"

You are more capable than you dreamed…

"Laundry," she answered.

"Laundry?"

"Yes. They were stupid questions. As if I have the money to be spending on some laundry service." Sobs.

"Why would they ask you about laundry?"

(The Four Square Laundry. You might expect an Active Service Unit of the I.R.A. to have acted on intelligence received, and not mete out fatally blind prejudice like the Loyalist death squads. You might expect that the same organisation that shot down the British Military Reaction Force's undercover operation to collect and forensically test clothes on the doorsteps of West Belfast, would know fine well that 'Jane', the woman who escaped when they riddled

Sapper Ted Stuart and comrades in that innocuous-looking laundry van, bore no physical resemblance to Mary McCandless.)

"I don't know, I don't know," she said as if she was being questioned all over again. Tears, helplessness, sobs escaping in great wracks.

"It's all right. You would've been in hospital when that all happened." Natalie came round the table and put her arms round Virgo.

"They hit me Natalie. I told them I didn't know what they were talking about... They beat me."

Natalie hugged the wetted face of poor Virgo, the mother of seven, into her breasts. "It's all right Mum. We'll be all right."

*

They told her Natalie had been hit by a car. Last night. To think that to get at her the Provos told her that her kid had been hurt.

It was a lie. They lied.

They sent Big Frank the Hangingtree's doorman into the club hall to interrupt her beloved bingo.

She'd no money left, but she'd gone out at her friend Christina's insistence—"I have a wee roughness and you can owe me a treat some other time, or pay me out of your winnings."

"Beady eyes of blue, fifty-two," was the last number she heard called from the makeshift stage before Big Frank broke the news.

"It can't be Natalie," she told the bouncer. "She's in the house looking after the kids."

Christina, always the lucky devil, was one number away from two lines across.

"There's people here to give you a lift to the Royal," Big Frank shrugged.

"Legs Eleven," was called.

"Who are they?" She was all in a rush, trying to gather her handbag, grab her coat, slip her good heels back on.

"How would I know? Come on out and see."

Heart racing, she got to her feet, shrugged at Christina, who'd bought her a whole book, a whole night's play— wasted.

"Do you want me to come with you?" Christina asked.

"No, no, no. You're on a lucky streak. Go on, win for me too." She pushed the book over the wooden fold-up table to her friend. Christina had done so much for her already, too much.

"I want to? I'll go."

"It's all right. Honestly," she lied, covering her fear as best she could, "It'll probably just be a scratch or something."

"Brighton Line. Fifty-nine," the caller announced.

Eyes down: her last sight of good fortune was Christina circling the last number: that was her two lines! Her friend should have held up a hand and yelled "—Two lines" but didn't, because…well…

She left promising, "I'll call you later…"

Christina nodded. "I'll be up to the Royal right after this, okay."

She hurried after Big Frank, who was holding the door to the hall open for her.

They went through into the lobby, Big Frank flanking her.

There was a girl of twenty there, who looked vaguely familiar, someone from the flats. The girl's beady-blue eyes narrowed, "Mary McCandless?"

"What's wrong with Natalie?"

"Hit-and-run darlin. No time to waste," the girl said, taking her hand, "Come on."

The girl led her outside. It was a bitter-cold night. The girl opened the back door of the car by the curb.

"What about the kids?" she said at the open door, "Who's looking after the kids?"

"Neighbours darlin," said the girl.

"Why was Natalie out?" she said, "She shouldn't have been out."

"How should I know?" the girl replied. "We can't wait all day—"

Thinking, *What about the kids?*

What about Natalie—if she's hurt badly, if she dies?

Christina came clattering through the hall doors into the lobby, and past Big Frank.

She just heard Christina call after them: "Hold on. This is silly. I'm coming with you Mary." But her friend wasn't coming, no—

Because she was suddenly pushed from behind; knocked off balance; the girl hustling, bundling her into the back seat, and jumping in behind her.

The car door slammed shut.

As the car drove away, the masked man in the passenger seat pointed a gun at her head. "Get down," he ordered her.

The girl with the beady blue eyes thrust a hood into her palms, "Put it on."

"What's going on? What about Natalie?"

The girl left-jabbed her hard in the mouth, stars, so quick, she didn't see it coming. "Put it on, shut up, and get down on the floor now. That's what's going on darlin."

Blood from a bust lip seeped into her mouth; scent, taste, of copper-tang rising in her nostrils raw and eye-watering as chlorine.

What about Natalie?

6

"Have you grassed up the Chain?"

Her bagged head sagged forward. By now the lungs in her body—that bound thing that was still holding her here—felt like they were full of sand. Her breathing had almost stopped. She barely heard the question, a mirage, yelled in her ear:

"Have you grassed up the Chain?"

A spasm shook her, the thirst for air, a volition not her own, her diaphragm quivering for it:

No, I'm not a British agent, I haven't grassed up the Chain!

Dunes. She saw dunes creeping seeping inland; in the bleaching-out haze of her mind's eye—a sighting of this liminal earth—but she was without understanding of the significance of this.

The Chain was a flexible system that allowed the Provos to hide caches of arms in Donard Flats and to move the guns, house-to-house when the Brits came raiding, which happened a lot since the G.H.Q. staff learned the hard lessons of the three-day long Falls Curfew: handguns were transported under infants in prams, old rifles were stored under the floorboards in kids' rooms and grenades were strapped under kitchen sinks.

"How did you grass up the Chain?"

She hadn't grassed up the Chain. But then again, she had

never taken part in it.

Two Provos, the same age as Martin, had come by last June to tell her: "We're protecting you, now fucking play your part, all right."

But she'd told them straight—"I'm not going to have blood on my hands boys, and that's that."

She could hear the beat, *boom, boom, boom* of surf somewhere near—

The sea?

The two boys threatened her of course: "We'll see about that you ungrateful Orange bitch," but for whatever reason, they hadn't come by again.

Thirteen-year-old Jean-Paul Hegarty, who Natalie called 'the spotty wee glipe next door', carried the guns past No 42. He always made a point of hacking and gobbing at the 'fucking Candles' door on his way back home.

Someone grabbed a hold of the Spar bag, her hair, her head, and shook it violently.

Her neck was shifting sand, no anchor for the head: it flopped around and then slumped forwards again.

Boom.

Boom.

"She's out cold," her interrogator said. "Who's got the water hey?"

You might expect what would come to be known as a 'nutting squad' to have water on hand to revive their prisoner in the likely event that torture led to unconsciousness, but this was no official Provisional debrief. No damage limitation exercise, where the collaborator informs 'the Unknowns' of information handed to the enemy to allow counter-intelligence measures to be set in motion. These were the early days of the Dirty War; that was not the order given.

Somebody was supplying the Brits with information on operations, this somebody. And this was a second punishment beating administered to get an admission of the truth.

Boom.

The windswept crusty beach at Greencastle, a pretend Sahara for her and her siblings. Holding her Daddy's hand while she shrieked and paddled and giggled naked in the stony foamy swash. Always safe in this man's hands. *You know you'll always be Daddy's little angel, don't you?* In the kiss of the Indian summer sun.

The interrogator sighed. "There's no water, is there—fucking marvellous."

To bring her to—

The best this four-man I.R.A. intimidation-not-interrogation squad could come up with to bring her to was the interrogator's half-tin of Tennents lager—one of those with the Lager Lovelies on the side.

Should you have grassed up the Chain—yes—but to Stormont's stormtroopers, the R.U.C.? The invading Brits—this handler who they demanded the name of?

"Where is the fucking transmitter you've been using, uh? Where'd you hide it?"

Creeping dunes. That covered everything up.

7

If Harold was here he'd save her. He'd protect her. With his Samurai sword, he'd slay their...defenders? He'd killed before. *Harold had killed people.* It was a thought that disturbed her some nights as she lay with him, his semen itching her inner thighs, and other nights when he'd been away on active service in Germany, Egypt, Korea, wherever in the world. *Harold had killed people. Harold could be killing someone for his living right now.*

"How many Japs did you kill in the war Dad?"

"Eight, that I know of son," he'd confided to Martin once; the seven-year-old was tugging on his knee in the kitchen. Dinner was over, she was doing the dishes, getting them out of the way as always.

"How'd you kill them Dad—did you shoot them?"

Her Harold was nothing if not a pragmatic man. He got up and showed the boy, coming up behind him and taking him round the neck and stabbing his big fingers into the boy's kidneys, just under the ribs, as if trying to rupture the renal artery.

Martin giggled as he was covertly killed.

War stories: that was apparently how the Chindits operated in Burma—"Call it Myanmar to show you're in the know son." Long Range Penetration. Behind enemy lines. Guerillas in the jungle mist. Take you from behind. With a knife. *Banzai!* No prisoners...

Except: for the purposes of interrogation and public execution, of course.

Yes, with his Samurai sword Harold would cut these woman-beating cowards down—

He had smuggled it to work to show it off to her. A hired handyman, and not allowed into the house proper with his boots on, he'd sneaked into the laundry room to see her—in his big toe-holed socks. She'd stopped ironing Mrs. Watson's starchy blouse, and let herself be impressed. "Look," he said, and pulled it out of an old army holdall. She looked. The scabbard was beautiful. And the *Katana* blade once drawn, a work of art. To take it he'd killed a Jap Captain—with his bare hands. He told her it was made of folded steel, folds and folds of the stuff. He let her hold it, so light, telling her the names of the parts of the sword—the *hasaki* was the cutting edge, this was the *ha*, this the *ji*, that is the *mono-uchi*—as she twisted it back and forth, effortlessly. The *kissaki*, or point, was the only one she could remember now. Because it contained the word 'kiss'. He did not tell her then that the Captain had been a small man, 5' 4" at most—to his 6' 3"; or that the sleeper hold he'd gripped him in was almost impossible to get out of; or that in his recurring dreams he felt like a hangman when he lifted that man right off his feet, and strangling him all the while, snapped his neck forward, crushing the vertebrae there like they were a child's. It would take twenty years for him to admit that to her, that first night when they were staying, the whole family outcast of East Belfast, thrown out of his mother's, on the floor in St. Joseph's Primary School, in the Ardoyne.

(The Loyalist pogrom of '69: Catholics from all over Belfast sought temporary refuge in schools and community halls, a desperate wait to be re-housed, after being intimidated out of their homes.)

Instead of telling her the whole truth and nothing but the murderous truth, he formally asked her out—"Would you Mary Smith like to accompany me to the pictures tomorrow night?" There she was standing over an ironing board holding the naked sword, the live sword in her right hand, blushing as she replied: "Yes, that would be nice, Harold McCandless."

McCandless—

She was trying the family name out for size. It fitted somehow; she'd decided on meeting his eyes that his surname would fit better than the anonymous Smith; wasn't that giddy as a Mills and Boon?

*

Yes. Harold would have saved her. If he'd been alive. *My Harold not alive?* It was a surprise every time, so strange to think of him as not there, and not away on another tour of duty not there, no, never there again. Passed-on.

He was coughing a lot. "Summer chest cold," he complained. Couldn't shake it. It was hard for him, for her, for them, to get any sleep with the racks of it shaking the double bed. She told him to cut down on the ciggies—he smoked thirty Woodbines a day, an army habit—and nagged him to go and see the doctor. He didn't go to see the doctor because he'd never been to see a doctor since the horror of the field hospital in Broadway, the jungle clearing that Major General Orde 'Orders is orders' Wingate, gung-tally-ho Chindit Commander, established two hundred miles behind Jap lines. The way Harold told and retold this old 'what doesn't kill you, makes you stronger' chestnut of his in the pub, any pub—he'd collapsed on a routine ambush patrol, going down with what he'd thought was exhaustion, starvation, dehydration, like everybody else out there, but what was really *beriberi*.

(The word *beriberi* means weakness-weakness in Singhalese.)

It was bloody awful, that Red Cross tent at the height of the North-Eastern monsoon of '44, with only two medics tending a hundred skeleton-men; little more than a morgue for bodies to rot in. Flies—some nightmare species, he never found out which—would lay their blinding eggs in some malarial Chinese's or Indian's eyes. He was one of the lucky ones. Somehow he got his thiamine shots, and kept his eyes open as best he could. He survived to be airlifted out under heavy fire. And he returned fattened-up to fight again in Operation Dracula, in '45, when half the Chindits did not, could not press home the victory.

His bog-standard anti-nagging response to her: "How can you—coming down with medical problems—push me to go to the doctor?" How dare she question his health? To a fighter like Harold his health was his authority.

The twelfth of August, the day of the annual Apprentice Boys March around the walls of 'the Maiden City' of Derry, was the day she put her foot down. They were having a cup of high tea—he couldn't get any building work with the war demolishing the streets—and he got the shakes. The tea went all over the place. "Casualty," she said, "I'm taking you to Casualty, no more excuses, no more arguments."

At the City Hospital that summer chest cold was traced to a dark shadow on his lung; the reason he couldn't shift it was that it was cancer. The X-rays showed it up, glowed it up, that rampant blackness in the grey hue of his lungs, locked in the glare-white of his ribcage. Other blood and sputum and lung function tests confirmed it. Diagnosis: Squamous Cell Carcinoma, or non-small cell lung cancer. "I can't believe it," he said. "It's not true."

She told him that it was okay, he was strong, he'd survive it: "You'll beat it." And she believed herself even if he didn't seem too convinced.

The Welsh oncologist informed them that that was the right fighting spirit, and instructed him that he was to stop smoking immediately, and they would operate as soon as an N.H.S. slot became available. "You do realise Mr McCandless it might be some time, the surgeons are working flat-out what with all the mayhem that's going on?"

Pneumonectomy: the whole left lung was exsected on 21st October '71, after a six-week wait in which he became weaker and weaker, so weak he couldn't even climb the stairs, breathlessness, or take cover on the floor when the daily gun-battles were waged outside their front door. "Why me? Why now?" he kept saying. "Why us?" She listened, without tears, with prayers: *Hail Mary, mother of God, the Lord is with thee...* Frankie and Martin and Natalie helped her move their double bed downstairs. She kissed him to sleep at night, like this—"I love you." A small puck on his cheek. "You'll be all right." A puck on his chin. "We'll get through this." Lips on his busted-bent nose, a growl, teeth gnawing the tip, making him laugh.

But the operation was not a success. And by then, radiotherapy was not a viable option. Tests revealed the cancer had attacked his lymph system and was running riot in his bone marrow. Their living room became his dying room. "If you'd just let me stay in the army woman, I'd have kept myself fitter..."

The word *beriberi* may have meant weakness-weakness in Singhalese, but bad as that disease was he told the kids that it was nothing compared to the wasting agonies of cancer. He joked: "If I get a new lease of life, a remission, I can update that old war story of my survival, can't I? What doesn't kill you makes you stronger."

"I'm going to die—like this," he said, as she was sponging him, a bed-bath. It was a cold late-November morning; the kids were at school. She tried to be sympathetic, she'd always wanted to be a nurse, but she was exhausted and could only manage a dulled caring by then. "It's all right for you," he was weeping, "You don't have to die like this."

Never mind the fight he put up, it withered him down to a yellow bag of bones by Christmas. The sheer speed of it, utterly terrifying. He couldn't control his bowels anymore. She had to sleep in Natalie's bed, the pair of them taking turns to watch over him night and day. He peed the bed worse than wee Eddie. But thankfully, he'd been prescribed morphine by that time and didn't know the half of it. "Don't die Harold McCandless," she smoothed his fever-matted hair, "I can't live without you. I can't and I won't."

Natalie was trying to feed him some mashed potato on Christmas Eve, when she realised he'd drifted into coma and wasn't responding. "Come back Dad? Dad? Daddy?"

"Please God, please," she prayed for a miracle in Christmas morning mass. They'd got Ruthie, poor simple smiling Ruthie who didn't understand what was wrong with Daddy, down from Muckamore Hospital for the holidays. So, all seven kids were in the chapel, singing the hymns, swallowing the Lord's body down, saying the responses— even Martin the Marxist-Leninist-Atheist; the whole time praying for the one same simple thing: *Save our Daddy, Jesus.*

But, she could feel it, the lack of him; had felt it since before dawn, on her vigil, had cried while putting the turkey in the oven for the family dinner, laying out the stockings on the hearth, his soul was already gone from this world.

His one lung continued to rasp till New Year's Eve, at ten past eleven, the officially recorded time of death, when according to Frankie, whose turn it was to sit with him, it simply stopped. "It just stopped Mum. Is he in Heaven now?"

*

This was why Harold could not save her. Then again, maybe even if he'd been alive and well, he couldn't have helped? He couldn't save them from the Loyalists a few years back, could he? What could one man, even a Chindit, do against a bloodthirsty mob like that?

Run.

That's what he did when he was forced to. At gunpoint, they'd pinned him to a wall, the local U.V.F. 'big hard men', not one of them six-foot tall. There were four of them lying in wait—in balaclavas.

Harold was drunk, in no fit state for a fight, and luckily for him at least, his best mate Sammy was with him. They'd been out to the pub for a pint and well, stayed for another, and another. Sammy, decent fella that he was, stepped up and put himself in the firing line: "Don't you shoot him. Harry there's a British soldier."

They told Sammy, "Shut up you fucking Taig-lover. We know where you live and all."

The U.V.F. man with the gun—the others had bits of two-by-four—put it to Harold's temple. "Get out, and take your Fenian bastards with you. You have till first light tomorrow." The pistol was cocked, the muzzle rammed into his skull, emphasis.

Run, Harold run.

Afterwards, after the flight to her mother-in-law's, she overheard Harold confiding to oul Brigid—how she hated it when he talked to his mother instead of her: "I never sobered up as fast in my life. The shock of it."

It shouldn't have come as a shock to him though. Early on the Eleventh Night of '66, three weeks after her hysterectomy, when her kids were all the more precious to her, a gang of kids had taken ten-year-old Frankie 'prisoner' and tied him to the top of their bonfire. They were going to light it and burn their 'I.R.A. Guy' when a mother, doubtless thinking—what if that was my own wee boy, came to the rescue.

When she'd been in hospital the following February—the thrombosis in her legs was back—Frankie had been set upon by teenage thugs and when Harold went to stop the kicking, they started on him. His guerrilla training, all that hitting and running, were the only things that got them out of that without broken bones. Her mother's minister, Reverend Hyde, visited her after that incident to offer some advice she refused to take—"Reconvert Mary. They'll leave you alone."

In the summer of 1968, every Saturday, 'Blood 'n' Thunder' bands would marshal right outside the McCandless' door. *Here lies a soldier, here lies a soldier, who fought and died for what he thought was best. Here lies a soldier, here lies a soldier, of the U.V.F!* The Lambeg drums would shake the window panes, the rattle of the snares would make the youngest bawl, and by the time the flutes started she'd made sure they were all safely away from any bricks and breaking glass and bricks. *Lero lero, lero lero, Lilli burlero, bullen a la... The Protestant Boys are loyal and true, though fashions are changed and the loyal are few...* Some of the bands' marchers and even some of the orange and blue uniformed band members would throw beer bottles and shout abuse—depending on how much Dutch courage had been had. *Hi! Ho! The Lily-O, the royal, loyal, Lily-O.* It was a far cry from when she'd watched the circus-like parades going by from on her Dad's shoulders, or was it was a near cry, too near to home?

Run. Get out.

With Sammy's help Harold lit out of the house, out the district the night of the warning. He didn't want to go but when they got safely back to No. 113, Sammy had told him in no uncertain terms: "Next time they'll do more than threaten you, they'll have you, and the kids. Remember Kieran Moss in number fifty-two?"

(Kieran, a Catholic welder at H&W, had been beaten to death by 'the boys' as he tried to defend his terrace house from a full-on frontal assault. His wife and five kids were stoned all down the road as they, on foot; were forced to leave him in the hall, bleeding his last into the frayed carpet.)

Sitting at the dining table, hands together: "Won't leave my kids. Won't leave Mary."

"Shh," she hushed, finger to mouth. She meant the walls were thin, that the neighbours who'd turned staunchly against them would hear, not to mention the kids upstairs.

Sammy toned it down to a whisper. "If you're gone, there's less chance of it turning ugly."

"No Sammy."

"He who fights and runs away, lives to fight another day. Tell him Mary."

So she summoned the courage to tell him to leave her and the family to the mercy of the mob. That was hard. She was quivering-scared. She wanted him there to protect her. That was one of the hardest right things she ever had to do. "I think you should go."

"I'll kill them. I'll kill them with my bare hands." It sounded as if he meant it, and she knew he could do it to one, had done it, but this was different, it was the threat of a man against a mob.

Running.

It went against everything he was, what he'd stood for, but he knew in his head they were right. If he got violent, that was it…

He got up from the table.

She kissed him goodbye, and taking a last kiss for good luck, out he went. "I'll phone you when I get to my mother's." The look on his face. She would never forget it. "Get a taxi out as soon as you can."

Run. Live to fight another day.

She woke Natalie and Martin up, to help her with the packing. "Just the things we need now. We'll have to leave the rest."

Martin helped her barricade the front door with the folded-down dining table and the chairs. "Fucking Orange bastards," he swore as he struggled to get everything in place so that it would hold, "Fucking Loyalist shiteheads." Normally she would have slapped him on the cheek for that sort of foul sectarian language, but she let it go. That night, it was the truth, and there was no denying it.

She put their few books, including the leather-covered Bible her Mum had given her on the day of her Catholic confirmation, on the bottom of the curtains at the front of the house—so they would hold the shards of glass when the windows shattered in. You live and learn.

Their portable worldly possessions were organised into four boxes, two bin-liners, and two suitcases, on the kitchen floor by four o'clock. Her eyelids were getting heavy. She decided to be safe and move all the kids into the girls' upstairs bedroom at the back of the house. The trouble would come from out front, in full view of the street, the U.V.F. making a public example of them. In her apron, she'd hidden their bread knife. Her fingers white-tight about the hilt.

(All U.V.F. men are volunteers, allowed to leave the Force at any time.)

At 'first light', as threatened, the siege of the house commenced. "Fucking I.R.A. bastards, get out!" A street's worth of milk bottles cracking and tinkling off the outside walls. "Youse don't belong here." She watched from the landing, through a crack in the door as stones punctured the front windows and puffed and plumed the lace curtains of her and Harold's bedroom like a ghost was rearing behind them. So many stones fizzed in that the books on the ledges were pushed off and fell to the floor. One of the curtains—a surprisingly delicate wedding present from her biggest brother, Malcolm, the Shorts trade unionist Unionist—was ripped away by a brick. She saw the windows of her home reduced to spider-webs, wrecked by more stones. The pelting clattered off the bedroom walls. Eddie started to wail. He tried to be a big brave boy like Martin but he was only five then, and the bangs and thwacks, so many, it seemed the house might fall down? Natalie wiped his crying eyes.

The barrage stopped. In the silence, *is that it? Please God.*

That was when the mob attacked the front door, battering

on it with cricket bats, wood splintering, but Martin's barricade held fast.

It was at that point she heard Sammy trying to placate the mob by yelling at them—"Harold McCandless has already left the area"—she heard later from her mother in a letter that he'd bravely strode out in front of the house, waving a white hanky—"it's just Mary and her kids in there."

That earned him a kneecapping.

Word is, they laid into him, knocked him do-lally and brought him round to the alley, her mother June wrote a week afterwards on her lavender-scented notepaper. *That's where it happened. His wife was saying they managed to reconstruct the knee so he might be able to walk, but he'll have a limp for the rest of his life and no mistake. Man's a hero but he'll have to watch his back.*

Mary had heard that shot. And the yelps of…Sammy, the fearful sound of a grown man crying. She got down and hugged Natalie and Eddie to her.

"What are we going to do Mum?" asked Natalie, her voice tight and high.

She had no answer other than, "Wait?"

The R.U.C. were called to the scene, along with Sammy's ambulance. There were only five of them but they lifted the siege, or 'street disturbance' as they would record it, enough to have a quiet word to her: "Mrs. McCandless, are you all right in there? Anybody hurt?"

"No, nobody's hurt, yet," she shouted back through the smashed upstairs windows.

"What do you want to do Mrs. McCandless? I'm not honestly sure we can protect you for any length of time here."

"Fascist wankers," Martin said loud enough to be heard below.

She who fights for her family and runs away, lives to fight another

day, was that it? No, it was more like—she wh..
them away, would live to see another day.

"We need to get out of here," she told them.

So the R.U.C. ordered a taxi. You might think that as t.. taxi didn't come for over an hour and a half, the cops might have driven them out of the area themselves, but no. You might expect at the very least that the police would have protected the family from the resurgent mob as the taxi arrived, but no. You could reasonably expect that those thugs who set upon the taxi, beating the windows with their fists, kicking dints into the doors and wings, terrorising the young family further, might have been arrested—at the very least for criminal damage of commercial property, they were as keen as mustard about pressing charges for that in West Belfast, but no.

This was the democratic time before civil rights.

The real world—

Where even now most liberal expectations and imaginations are snuffed out by law or outlaw, by sheer force.

8

The bag was stuck to the left side of her face. Coagulation, excessive clotting, that was the curse of her condition: thrombosis, aggravated by thrombocytosis. The interrogator had to peel it off, provoking a rare moment of squeam-ishness for him. Tearing at the plastic membrane with one hand, holding the Tennents can, his fourth tonight, in the other.

The hardened blood gave way with a bit more jigging. The cast-off bag, freed of the weight of misery, wafted gently to the floor.

He gripped her matted scalp, jerked her head up, and was confronted with her face. "Aw, shite."

She was blue, where she hadn't bled. Her face was fucking bluer than his Ma's bathroom.

It was only supposed to be a warning. If she dies on you…

"Like, what's wrong Donal?" asked one of the squad, the new boy, sixteen, from Andersonstown, *was it Jim, slim Jim?* (Internment: fired up by Bloody Sunday, they came in full of 'Up the 'Ra!' and went to prison without trial so fast he couldn't keep track of their names.)

Donal Keenan, her Volunteer interrogator of a troubled twenty-one years of age, just pointed. "Look, the bitch is…aw fuck."

(All I.R.A. men are volunteers, free to leave the Movement at any time.)

Quickly, it was his ability to move quickly, think decisively, drink copiously, that'd saved him many times on the street barricades, he poured the Tennents over her forehead. The lager frothed down her face, turning it green. No response.

Her lips were greying.

He dropped the tin, and slapped her, lightly mind this time, on the cheeks. *Come on you bloody cow, you bloody Brit-loving cow—he'd be for it with the Brigade staff if she couped it?*

Pulling her eyelids back, all white: her pupils were rolled right back. Fixed and dilated. And the blood-veins round the edges, fading pink. She was out of there big-time.

Hypoxia, poxy hypoxia: this isn't happening. This wasn't supposed to happen.

"Mary! Waken up will you?" There was a homely innocence to those words, were they really his?, like he was shouting them upstairs to get his big sister Mary up for school, after the milk-round was done. That was his job. And it was a job and a half to get her big lazy bones up. She never once said thanks either.

Two-fingered probing under her jaw, feeling for a pulse in her carotid. None. Wait a minute. There was one. It was very weak.

"We have to get her untied, now."

The three others, laggards every one when it came to getting something done, lent a hand with the ropes—

Bobby Cairns, mindless mass of Marxist muscle that he was, fiddle-undid the binding round the arms and back of the chair.

Jim used a Swiss Army knife to cut free the hands.

Declan 'Dec" Laverty, a dab hand of a driver whose brother had been blown up by his own black-stuff bomb earlier that year, borrowed the knife to do the feet.

The plastic bag. Fuck. If only the stupid bitch hadn't run off with my hood last night—black pillowcases thick enough were hard to come by—this wouldn't have happened.

They laid her down on the stone floor.

"Mary? Mary? Mary McCandless!"

9

Mary!—she heard her name being called. From somewhere. Up above? Down below? Not knowing where here was, or there. *Mary?* Loud, jarring, on all sides of her. A powerful voice, male, loud and angry as God.

Harold?

But Harold was gone. There was no one to call her back now… *Back from where?*

The coffin lowered down and down into the slick red clay of Lisburn Cemetery.

The McCandless plot reopened for him, a welcome home from his ancestors, a decent Christian burial. With everybody still alive, surviving him, gathered there to say goodbye. Over a hundred and fifty souls. Family and friends like Sammy, and some old war comrades in mothballed uniforms. Brigid's proud tearful tribute in the service—"He was a good man, like you know. He fought the good fight. It was cancer, 'the Big C', what could you do against that? Even my boy, my big best boy couldn't beat that." (This was the same oul Brigid who did not speak to her son for two years after he married that plain-looking Proddy bitch—"You'll regret it for the rest of your life, God forgive you because I won't.")

Not one of the mourners leaving after the funeral mass, everyone there at the end, glad in a way that he was gone, no more suffering any more pain.

Standing closest to the graveside, on the very edge, with her own big best boy Martin holding her there: her eyes following the descent into the red earth.

Thinking—*Didn't the name of the first man God created, Adam, mean 'Red earth'.*

But Eve, she didn't know what Eve meant. The Bible does not tell us so. Sunday School neither? Sole trace memory: *Eater of the fruit of the tree of the knowledge of good and evil, temptress, mother of sin?*

Eyes following the coffin down till it reached its final resting place, such a long way down, vertigo swoons.

Thinking, a melodrama of prayer, rather than feel the loss: *Father, forgive my sins, and lead me not into temptation?*

The temptation to fall, no, to leap in there—oh God, the temptation. Life afterlife. But she, daughter of Eve, did not belong there. She had sinned somehow, without knowing, if that was a sin; and Harold had got cancer; if that could be a sin that condemned a woman to living a Hell, could it, could it really?

"Dust to dust, ashes to ashes. In sure and certain knowledge of the resurrection of our Lord Jesus Christ..."

The priest, in his blackest vestments, nodding at her.

She looked at the red earth in her black-gloved palm. Red clay to red clay. She dropped it into the hole; the stones in it rattling like a crow's claws skittering on the coffin lid, too much—

It was what happened to Ruthie wasn't it Lord? It was not looking over her that second in the pram, when everything turned bad, that was why she was being punished so much. Martin pulled her back from the brink as her knees gave out.

Mary?—the by-now faint voice calling her back.

Whose was that corpse down there in that box? What if it was her body? Would all these people, so sorry she was gone, be gathered around her grave here to grieve for her? No. There would only be her close family. All her former friends from East Belfast would not come because she was a 'Turn'. And Christina was her only friend in the West.

Let me go.

Patches of whiteness, memory's cosmetic, crème bleach spilling over the memory of Ruthie's injury.

Let me go.

10

Donal got down on his knees beside the bitch. The floor was chilling.

Top-to-toe survey as she lay there in that thin rose-patterned dress: three scalp wounds, rough tears, tissue damage, capillary bleeding, coozes; lacerations to both eyes, above, on the brows and around the edges of the orbits; contusions to the left side of her jaw, cheek, ear; split lips; possible fractured nose; bleeding gums; swelling on the left forearm, possible fracture of radius. Chafing of the wrists, upper arms, due to the ropes, and, bruising to legs. And the right foot, possible crush fractures of three toes.

It doesn't look good, does it?

But it wasn't excessive. None of the injuries Donal, it was mainly him (though Bobby had put in a few blows for show), had inflicted were fatal. He took care to be precise. Knew the limits. First Aid training with the St. John's Ambulance '68—'69 stood him in good stead.

You'll have to save her. But the hypoxia? Within three minutes, brain damage. More, and it was curtains. The question was—how long had she been this blue?

They'd tortured him, the Brits and R.U.C. Special Branch, after he got arrested without charge in September '71. Dragged out of a friend's at midnight in his pyjamas. Beaten black and blue with batons. Shoved into a Pig. Taken to

Palace Barracks. Stripped. Hooded. Subjected to a torrent of abuse. "We know you're a fucking Provo cunt." Put in a boiler suit. Handcuffed. Placed in a cell for the night. Woken up. Beaten to raw meat around the feet. Release the next morning with contempt, but without charge. A limping out of there. An oath sworn, vengeance: *If the Brits were using torture, beatings, white noise, stress positions, sleep deprivation, what about it? Talk about justification, talk about retaliation. Aye. What about the Geneva Convention? Talk about old Compton, the Brown Tribunal. Talk about Diplock and his leaked Torturers' Charter if you've got anything to say.*

Oisin, his big fucking pretentious brother, Ma's favourite intellectual, now studying Medicine at Trinity, was the one who'd advised him to give it a go—"You can help save someone's life, there's nothing like saving someone's life. You're a hero in that moment, and it lives on, that feeling, forever, because life's so so precious." (This, despite the fact that Oisin had never yet saved someone's life, for real.)

I could be court-martialled for this balls-up. Take two in the back of the head, a double-tap.

"What are you going to do like?" asked Jim.

Donal crouched over the stupid cow. He leaned his face over her mouth to listen—if he could just feel her breath on his stubbled cheek—ten seconds counted—he couldn't. No chest movement either.

She still had a weak pulse though.

Unconscious casualty, not breathing, heart beating—try mouth-to-mouth.

'Torture' and 'inhuman and degrading treatment' is a necessary factor in war. This is what Joe his boss—whose younger brother Kevin owed his life to Donal—would drill into him over and over, positive reinforcement, 'grooming

60

him for bigger things'. "Winning a guerrilla war is all about effective intelligence gathering son. When all else covert fails, you have to interrogate people. Be surgical, be clinical, and be cynical if you want to get on."

He, who was all of these things; as well as being "a terrible disappointment to the family" (that was how Oisin put it when he'd told him he'd joined 'the Movement'); as well as being one of the few people he knew to have even skim-read the Geneva Convention of 1949 (knowledge he was to use to his advantage in 1981 when he was a Blanket Man, on Dirty Protest for Special Category Status in the H.M. Maze Prison doing life for the murder of an R.U.C. Reserve Constable); this revolutionary he, tilted her head back, stuck his fingers into her throat to clear the airway.

Clear.

Mouth-to-mouth ventilation works on the principle that there is twenty-one percent of oxygen in the air. When a human inhales, oxygen uptake is around five percent so upon expiry, sixteen percent is left. This is sufficient to keep a casualty alive if 'the kiss of life' is performed.

I have to stick my lips on this Brit-lover, Jesus fuck, the things you have to do!

Donal gave her a breath; inhaling away from her face, exhaling into it, nose pinched, lips forming a seal; then another.

He checked for a pulse. *Okay.*

Ten more breaths: one, two, three, *close the nostrils eejit*, four, five, six, *try to inhale deeper*, seven, eight, nine, ten.

Check pulse?—yes.

Ten more breaths.

"Is she going to make it," asked Jim.

Ten more breaths.

If the worst comes to the worst, you'll have to call in the marker and hope—

He was owed. Kevin the C/O's brother had been shot in the hand by the 3rd Para in the three days of house-to-house fighting in the Lower Falls. The high velocity full metal jacket S.L.R. round bored a neat hole into his wrist and deflected off his carpal bones, up his forearm deforming all the nerves, sinews, muscles, white-hot lead exploding out of his triceps in a plume of fuzzy pink, arterial spray.

In that moment, Donal the hero had been there, a medic under fire, tending to the man down in the street, applying full-on pressure on the brachial pressure point, holding the limb up, struggling like mad to get a field dressing on it before bleed-out.

Tracer, lines of murderous velocity fizzing bright up the street, by him…

A moment after the dressing was on, he'd dragged the man into cover, a terrace house; the Brits had already been and trashed through it, the front door kicked-in, the tenants absent, in hiding or captured.

He'd kept the casualty alive, through teeth-jittering shock, in the tiny kitchen, till other Volunteers were able to break the curfew and smuggle him out of the area and down for an unregistered G.S.W. treatment in Dundalk. He lived on did Kevin, Joe's younger brother, on the run, paralysed from the elbow down, but still thankful.

What did Oisin the snob know about anything, down there safe as houses in fucking Dublin? While there was a war raging up here. A war, and no mistake. Their own people being attacked by the age-old Imperial enemy, forced to flee their homes, robbed, killed. What did anyone in the unFair City know—they should be ashamed to call themselves Irish?

Check pulse?—fading.

*

Geneva Convention IV, relative to the Protection of Civilian Persons in Time of War. Article 3 (1): Persons taking no active part in the hostilities, including members of the armed forces who have laid down their arms and those placed hors de combat *by sickness, wounds, detention, or any other cause, shall in all circumstances be treated humanely, without any adverse distinction founded on race, colour, religion or faith, sex, birth or wealth, or any other similar criteria. To this end the following acts are and shall remain prohibited at any time and in any place whatsoever with respect to the above mentioned persons:*

a: violence to life and person, in particular murder of all kinds, mutilation, cruel treatment and torture

b: taking of hostages

c: outrages upon personal dignity, in particular, humiliating and degrading treatment

d: the passing of sentences and the carrying out of executions without previous judgement pronounced by a regularly constituted court, affording all the judicial guarantees which are recognised as indispensable to civilised peoples

11

Mmm. Harold's beery tongue in her mouth, licking round hers, thick and hard, probing, a pleasurable choking as he entered her on their bed. Slow thrusts, her pelvis rocking into each, filling her up.

The image fading, gone: amnesiac whiteness. *CAUTION: When using hydrogen peroxide to lighten excess dark hair...*

But he was home on leave!

"Let her be herself tonight, eh, for once?" her mother had berated and bribed her teenage sister Sarah into baby-sitting Ruthie Ruthie Ruthie and one-year-old Martin for them. They'd gone all suited and dressed up, it took her two hours to make herself up—red, red lipstick, hairspray on the bob, toning the foundation just right in the mirror, trying on her two possible dresses with her one pair of heels. When she was ready the taxi, "a real lady's treat for a real lady", was waiting to take them to the Flo', at Belfast Castle, for a hot summer night of dancing to Dave Glover's showband.

Twelve years older or not, he could dance could Harold, sweep you up, breathless, and take you round the floor with a quickstepping grace, a natural rhythm. And jive, even though he claimed it was "too new-fangled for an old codger like him", he'd fast-foxtrot you round, swing you into a hair-swirling twirl and out with ease, rocking around the clock.

After the Queen had been played; *God save our gracious*

Queen, long live our noble Queen, God save the Queen, Harold, a royalist popehead, singing hand on heart sincere. (Most Catholics on Nationalist principles understandably tended to avoid venues that played 'The Queen'.)

And after the Glover band was packing up their horns and guitars, and the younger ones, paired off, were gathering around the pond outside to say their goodbyes, or as Harold put it "hellos to the electric duck", a wink at her…

(It was an old joke. The electric duck may have been a tawdrily painted plastic swan that glided around in the Floral Hall pond on submerged rails; in show band circles though, saying hello to it had become rhyming slang for an invite to heavy petting, and in some cases, even sex in the Castle grounds.)

Afterwards, Harold would lead you away from the bus; escorting you hand in hand down the steep Castle steps towards the gates. There, in the dying light, on the slopes of the Black Mountain, overlooking the divided city, he'd share a few swigs of his hip-flask with you, straight, throat-searing Paddy whiskey.

On the tram back into Belfast, a rickety ride, he'd talk about all the exciting exotic things he'd seen on his travels, since he'd been gone, away. The way old Bavarians in peaked caps got tore into three litre jugs of beer at the Munich Beer Festival, you know Hitler must have done that himself… The Strait of Hormuz, from the top of the Rock, reflecting the sunset, dying Gibraltar rosy red, and wishing you were there so bad… A boot-stomping changing of the guard at Buckingham Palace, *Christopher Robin went down with Alice*. She could see them, as if through a tunnel, all the adventurous colours of this second hand world of promises and passionate experiences, then—

CAUTION: Do not expose areas to which the product has been applied to intense or prolonged sunlight for a period of twenty-four hours after application.

Two shadows standing outside the City Hall. A kiss under a streetlamp with this familiar stranger before they got the last tram home; romantic, fresh, new, the way it somehow should be: his lips caressing, teasing at her lower lip, making her lean into him with a moan. His warm hand slipping into her coat, gliding up her blouse to her breasts, cold-nipple-pert. She giggles like a girl, "Where's this electric duck of yours soldier?"

CAUTION: Do not apply if skin has cuts or abrasions.

CAUTION: There are happy times in life. But they are so few, and far between. And the distance, why could you never see that far ahead, to the next one?

The babysitter paid a bob or two—"Thank you and goodnight sister Sarah." Wink-wink.

Little baby Ruthie left in her pram—not to be put down in the cot till after the romance—frees her tiny arms and legs out of the tucked-in pink blanket and crawls up over the rim.

CAUTION: Do not use near the eyes or sensitive regions. If the product comes into contact with the eyes, rinse with cold water immediately. Keep out of the reach of children.

12

He'd traced the sternum with his left hand. Two fingers up from where the ribs meet the breastbone, he placed his right hand on her chest. *Joe'll do his nut—he'll say you let him down.* He leaned forward and began the chest compressions, bringing his weight down on her, pressing in the flesh the required one to two inches. His Second World War Colt .45 fell out of the back of his jeans and clacked on the floor. Reflexes, even this numbed: he nearly jumped out of his skin. When he looked back, fear-flight, saw the antique, and then taking a gander over at the others, seeing Bobby look disapprovingly (the other two were in no mood for slagging), he left it lying there. Admittedly, it was stupid carrying it like that, even with the safety on: last month a fella in the Car Bomb had blown off half his arse and an ankle doing the selfsame thing. *No time to worry about that though, small beer in comparison to this stuff-up.*

Jim: "Is she going to make it? Do you need a hand?"

"Do you know C.P.R.?" he said.

"What?"

"Never mind." In full C.P.R., (Cardiopulmonary Resuscitation) the correct performance rate was one hundred compressions a minute. Two breaths. Followed by fifteen compressions.

No pulse?

No chest inflation?

Repeat the procedure until the patient shows signs of recovery; or help arrives—right, like he could call an ambulance; or you are physically unable to continue.

Come on you bitch you. Breathe.

13

The world dyed-out, white-golden light, dazzling. *The sun so close?* Face-to-face with the sun. Yet unhurt by the sheer blasting beneficence of radiance ahead. No heat. Although— is there a burning far off like when the psychiatrist put those electrodes to her temples? Bursting light. Pulses of rapturous white light. And the light is alive. Enveloping her, passing through her, waves. A star-swirl of presences, acknowledging hers. Here was love. Here was joy. Here was bliss. Here was knowledge. Here was oneness, connection in uncertain space. The essences she could not find before... When? The other time, pills taken. Before—*It was not your fault that our Ruthie was brain-damaged. And it wasn't mine either. It just happened. How many times do I have to tell you that before you'll believe me?* Feelings flowing, not words spoken—was this forgiveness that came to her? *Harold? Is that you?* And a rush of the pure light shone through her, as if all the love she had given to him was coming back to her all at once. Thrilling her with the ecstasy of the eternal, a promise kept. *The rules of the game are changing. It's time to put yourself first Mary. Overcome your hesitancy, use that quiet determination and reach out for your goal.* She did not believe in astrology but ah, the ease of knowing him forever. Never being lost again. Dying but never dying, rising up like Jesus. *This must be God?* All her prayers had not been in vain. *God is love.* She knew it, she knew she was not alone. The voice of authority, from On High: *Let go*. And she nearly obeyed Him...

Except: for wee Eddie, she might have let the light take her.

Except: for her debt to Ruthie.

Except: for the others, the love she had for all of them; she couldn't leave them to fend for themselves, *it isn't right Lord.*

*

A small shrine, the kind of miniature grotto there are more of in the Free State, erected by the edge of a road, or was it a car park—yes, a car park. Built up, separated from the spiky swishing dune-grass, with sea-smoothed rocks. There were three figurines stood in this little sacred place. The biggest, Jesus, pointing both hands at what looked like a shotgun wound in his chest but what was really the sacred heart glowing there. The second largest was Mary, she was praying, white shawl over her head. The third was Joseph, holding his son, or rather the son of God, proudly, riding up on his carpenter's shoulders. There were flowers in front of the shrine, white lilies. Jesus, Mary and Joseph. And a small marble plaque that was respectfully painted with the words:

> *In memory of our beloved Mother*
> *Mary McCandless missing since*
> *7th December 1972, believed murdered*
> *by the I.R.A. and buried on this beach.*

14

There!

A quiet gasp had issued from her lips. *Seven...* He stopped compressions on: *eight*. He was out of breath. He was sweating like a bastard, an all-over lather. He had not been far from giving up, due to being unable to continue.

Check pulse?

Faint, fluttering-rapid, but there. In the carotid!

And yeah, her breasts, rising in weak waves. The bitch was breathing again. He'd got her back. *Aw thank fuck like*, he'd got her back.

"You," he pointed at Jim, "Get your bony ass over here."

Jim the new boy strutted over.

"Grab a hold of her ankles and lift her legs up."

Jim did as he was told, squatting, pulling the legs up and apart. Hunched. A confused look on his face. Not knowing what to do with them? "Is she alive?"

The practise of raising the legs above the level of the heart was to combat shock—by means of gravity the blood in the arteries and veins would drain out of the legs quicker and into the body's core, the vital organs that needed heat and oxygen most—and be more likely to stay there. Blood in the extremities was not a priority at this point in recovery.

"Aye. Now stand up straight man. Hold them at waist level. To your waist, yeah? And don't let go."

As Jim pulled her short legs up, hoisting her pelvis off the floor, the rosy summer dress slipped down her varicose-blue-veined legs to bunch at her waist, exposing the pallid pink folds of her vagina, and further up, her hysterectomy stitch-scar, cut deep into a loose track of stretch-marks.

"Quare hairy minge, hasn't she?" Jim the new boy joked, nodding down between her limp legs.

Still on his knees, Donal looked at the cunt, and laughed. Sharply, a single retort: Ha!

Ha-ha-ha: Bobby laughing enough for all of them, gulders that carried through the air, molecule vibrating molecule, the whole way through the safe house, and into the cold dark street, to where an old woman was walking by with her toy poodle, wittering "Come on Sooky, no pee-pee there, good girl." The old woman was wearing an N.H.S. hearing aid but it was not switched on so she did not hear anything from the derelict house. It seemed everyone living near to that house of pain suffered from the same condition.

The sense of relief, *Jesus.*

Do I need a ciggy, or what? He reached into his bomber-jacket pocket and drew out the black pack of J.P.S.

Lighting-up was never so good.

I.R.A. STATEMENT OF APOLOGY ON 'THE DISAPPEARED', ISSUED 29/4/1999

Eighteen months ago we established a special unit under the command of one of our most senior officers to ascertain the whereabouts of a number of people executed and buried by Oglaigh na hEireann *(I.R.A.)* approximately twenty years ago.

These burials took place prior to an Army Council directive that the body of anyone killed by Oglagh na hEireann should be left for burial by their relatives. This issue has caused incalculable pain and distress to a number of families over a period of many years.

Despite many complicating factors which have both hampered and protracted this investigation, including the lapse in time, changes in leadership, and the deaths of both members and former members of Oglagh na hEireann who were involved, we can now conclude this inquiry.

We believe we have established the whereabouts of the graves of nine people, some of whom were members of Oglagh na hEireann executed for activities which put other Oglagh na hEireann personnel at risk or jeopardised the struggle. Information regarding the location of these graves is now being processed and will hopefully result in the speedy retrieval of the bodies.

As we have previously stated, we are not responsible for all those previously listed in the media as having gone missing in the last thirty years. We are responsible for those we have acknowledged today and their families have all been notified.

In initiating this investigation our intention has been to do all within our power to rectify an injustice for which we accept full responsibility and to alleviate the suffering of the families. We are sorry that this has taken so long to resolve and for the prolonged anguish caused to the families.

PART TWO

15

The light, the light falling away, the fading of the light…

The beat, *boom-boom*, *boom-boom*, of her heart.

That there bloody beat that wouldn't ever stop? (The Lover.)

Boom-boom, fast.

Perceived as a singularity, as if the muscle contractions, spasmodic fibrillations, were being funnelled along a tunnel. And somewhere in the darkness, she heard distant devilish cackling. *Sent back for the kids.* An invisible evil, mocking her.

It isn't your time.

It isn't your time yet. (The Mother.)

*

Thrombosis, or 'trombonesis' as wee Eddie pronounced it on his first hospital visit, is the formation of a solid clot of blood in an artery or vein. A clot—thrombus—forms when blood comes into contact with a wound, or a damaged vessel wall. This sets off a chemical chain reaction called haemostasis or coagulation. The doctor had explained it all very methodically to her. He was a young Indian, keen to utilise the English language and his knowledge of human anatomy and pathology. But despite his patience, she only remembered bits of it. Platelets bonding. Her 'enemy enzyme', thrombin. The frightening clinical terms, 'Deep Vein Thrombosis', and 'Pulmonary Embolism'. The symptoms she was to look for in future: redness in the affected area, pain, swelling, mild fever, rapid heartbeat, sudden coughing, joint pains. "You can't expect the female body, wonder that it is madam, to produce so many children without paying a price, yes?"

Harold had insisted she go when he saw the calf on her left leg. The veins on the inner curve were swollen and blue, tenderised web-like spirals. A varicose vein—one of only two she had then—was where the clot gathered into a big lump, under the skin, an internal bruise of sorts. It looked so ugly she didn't like him to see it. But, when she came out of the bath, with a towel wrapped around her middle, he was waiting for a hug. "Jesus, what's wrong with your leg?" They took a taxi to the Royal with Eddie hugging his big Disney colouring-in book and crayons all the way, bugger the expense.

The Indian doctor, he could have been Pakistani for all she knew, had taken her complaint very seriously. "Are you pregnant Mrs. McCandless?"

"No."

"Have you ever had this before?"

"Yes, but a hot bath normally cured it."

The doctor nodded vigorously. "Yes, yes, have you been coughing at all?"

"No."

"No blood?"

"No."

"Any chest pains?"

"No."

"Good, good." Interrogation over.

In the waiting room Harold and the twins sat and worried for her. Eddie wouldn't stop crying. "Son, look, come over here till we do Donald Duck. That's a boy."

The tests: flexing her leg upwards—pain. "Indeed, yes."

Down to another department: local anaesthesia of her foot, injection of radioactive dye, an X-ray of the vein-web in her leg.

Diagnosis: "You have a D.V.T. madam."

"What?"

"Deep Vein Thrombosis. This is a potentially fatal condition if it is not stabilised. You'll have to stay in overnight at least, for treatment and observation. We'll start you on Heparin right away. This will thin your blood and dissolve the clot in your system before anything serious occurs. Nurse?"

What could have happened—

Pulmonary Embolism (where the clot travels to the lungs and blocks the blood supply from the pumping heart which is starved of oxygen and dies.)

Or Coronary Thrombosis (heart attack).

Or a stroke (clot on the brain).

And what could have happened, could happen still, because of an underlying blood disorder she had called thrombocytosis. Primary thrombocytosis (or essential thrombocythemia) is a disorder of the blood which results in the body producing a surplus amount of platelets. Platelets (thrombocytes) are blood cells that stick together on chemical cue helping the blood clot. There is no known way to prevent thrombocytosis. Treatment: Warfarin, a blood-thinning drug, has some beneficial effects on patient prognosis.

"You must be very careful with yourself Mrs.

McCandless. Watch for symptoms…I mean, watch out for the symptoms, yes?"

*

Yea verily, she felt the Devil himself; could hear the prince of the power of the air, laughing at her.

But deliver us from evil, for thine is the kingdom the power and the glory forever and ever. Amen.

"Primary thrombocytosis, Mrs. McCandless, is a single disease entity the cause of which is unknown. The symptoms are headaches, dizziness, weakness, confusion, redness or tingling in the hands and feet, itchiness, bruising, bleeding, bloody stools. Yes?"

The Devil.

The Devil. May you be dead a month before the Devil hears of it.

Please God, help me think it isn't my time yet, Amen.

16

Birchill: a riot-torn slum neighbourhood off the Lower Falls. That was where Natalie and Frankie had split-up, out searching, UP THE 'RA! BRITS OUT! sprayed on the walls in red over older white graffiti like SMASH STORMONT, JOIN YOUR LOCAL UNIT, Ireland for the Irish, because that was where the Brits said they'd found her the night of the first abduction.

*

For all her life was worth Christina had rushed around to Flat 42—this was of course after the car sped off from the Hangingtree with Mary in it. A battering on the door. "Natalie!"

Babysitting Natalie had dozed off but she woke with a jump.

"Natalie, open up!" Christina, distraught and out of breath, asked her, "You all right?"

She said, "Yes, fine. Why?"

So Christina told her what had happened, about the hit-and-run ruse, without really knowing anything about what had happened.

Natalie got her coat on. *Maybe the girl got the wrong person, the wrong identity, the wrong girl and the wrong mother?*

The pair of them went straight up to the Royal, leaving the kids in the care of a confused Frankie.

But, "Sorry miss", the nurses had not treated the injuries of anyone by the name of McCandless that night, and there had been no reports of a hit-and-run accident, let alone one involving a young woman.

Returning, fast in the falling frost of that bitterly cold clear night, Natalie convinced herself: "It's a mistake. She'll be back at home waiting for us."

Christina agreed, but she couldn't help thinking about the way Mary had been pushed into the car.

When Mary wasn't found safe and sound back at the flat, Natalie got really worried. "Where is she? What's happened to her? What could she be doing out this late?"

Frankie picked up on this: "What's going on?" he demanded to know, thirteen was more than old enough to know things, serious things.

So Natalie filled him in, nervously, saying as little as she had to.

His comment: "You don't think she's gone nutso again, do you?" He drew spirals on his temples.

"You have no respect Franklin McCandless," Natalie scolded, "None." Though inwardly it was anxiety, not anger, that she felt mostly—the psychiatric nurses had told her to help her Mum avoid stress as much as possible: excess stress would lead to depression.

"Sorry," said Frankie, with a shrug that declared he wasn't really. Granny Brigid insisted it wasn't his fault his Mum was barmy.

"Try not to worry dears." Christina made them both a

cup of tea. They turned on the radio, down low, so as not to wake Eddie upstairs. *And good ol' boys are drinkin' whiskey 'n' rye…*Don McLean's *American Pie*. And lips dry and tacky, slurped at another cup of tea…

"—there have been two gun attacks on soldiers in Ardogne. A soldier had been critically injured. And finally, Apollo 14 has safely blasted off from Cape Canaveral on its way to the moon. Presenting a smile. That was the news from the B.B.C. Good evening."

When the clock ticked all the way to one, Christina said, "I think we have to phone the police."

"Aye right!" said Frankie. "They'll not come down here. In case you're forgetting, this is still a no-go area, barricades or no barricades."

('Operation Motorman', the biggest mobilisation of the British Army since the Suez Crisis, unleashed on 1st August, had bulldozered all barricades from the streets of Belfast and Derry in a failed effort to eradicate these 'no-go areas' and crush the revolutionary spirit of '69.)

More strong cups of tea—it was char all right. America playing: *A Horse With No Name*. And Neil Young, *Heart Of Gold*. Followed by *Rocket Man*. *Witchy Woman*. *Bang A Gong (Get It On)*. Listening to the procession of pop hits. Then, a protest song: Bob Dylan's *Blowin'in the Wind*. Nobody saying anything for ages…

A caffeine and adrenalin edge: *her Mum was such a home-bird, she never went out, why, why her?*

At ten minutes to three, there was a single loud thump on the door. "Army. Open up."

Fearful, Natalie and Christina and Frankie went to the door. They didn't open it.

"What do youse wankers want?" Frankie shouted out.

(His anti-Brit politics fanatical since the night, three months back, when his mate Gerard had been shot in the face with a baton round. Gerard had to stay in exile over the Border till the New Year when the Scots Guards' tour would be finished. They were only throwing stones at the Saracen tanks for the news cameras—like everybody else.)

"We have a Mrs. McCandless back at barracks. This is the correct address?" Posh, public school English.

"What have you done with her?" Frankie launched himself at the door and the enemy beyond.

Christina grabbed a hold of his arm and pulled him back behind her. "Let's see what they have to say son."

Frankie was fuming.

Natalie opened the door to a tall but fatigued-looking Second Lieutenant of the Scots Guards.

"Are you Mrs. Mary McCandless' daughter by any chance?"

Natalie nodded.

"Well, we think we have your mother down at Prince Albert Street. A patrol found her wandering around the Birchill area in a very distressed condition."

"After you beat her up, no doubt?" Frankie shouted.

"Shut up Frankie," Natalie told him.

The Second Lieutenant was disdainful in his reply: "She has been beaten, but not by the British Army, I can assure you. Whoever did it, took her shoes and her coat."

"She must be half-frozen in this cold?" Christina said.

"Quite. Would you like us to give you a lift to the barracks? We have a Pig waiting at the end of the street."

"No, thanks," said Natalie. You couldn't accept an offer from the Brits, even if you wanted to run the risk of being ambushed and killed along with them. People would talk, then they would act.

"Right then, we'll be off. I hope your mother is, well, is all right."

"Yes," said Natalie.

So they'd gone to collect her Mum. Christina and her, carrying a pair of slippers, and her old Marks and Sparks raincoat.

You could see your own breath-mist as you walked through it.

You could see the moon and all the stars in the night sky, not a cloud.

You could see hoar frost, crystal-glitter on the rutted and cracked paving stones.

"It must have been the 'Ra?" Natalie guessed correctly half-way there.

But Christina said, "For God's sake Natalie, why would they be interested in hurting someone like Mary?"

At the fortified barbed gates of the barracks was where they first heard her screams. Hysterical sobbing. Inside: a handlebar-'tached sergeant in a kilt was sitting with her in the emptied N.C.O.'s mess, trying to comfort her, take the black hood from out of her hands, find out who'd done this to her, but she was uncontrollable, inconsolable till Natalie came and hugged her.

Christina hugged her too, was so guilty she hadn't come along when she should have. "What happened Mary? Who did this to you?"

She couldn't tell them. In their arms, choking back the sorrow and the hurt and the sorrys-for, she tried to get herself together. She took a cup of strong tea from the sergeant and supped and sobbed at it quietly.

Natalie stroked her mother's hair; a large clump of hair

came away in her soothing fingers; hiding that with—"I love you"—and a flick of the wrist.

The sergeant offered to lay on a lift home, but Christina politely-as-she-could declined, "No, thanks."

"Here Mum, we brought you these," said Natalie and gave her the slippers and the raincoat.

She put them on, wincing with the pain in her chest from the beating. Small sniffs of breath, attempted composure. Only then did she release the hood from her grip...it dropped to the floor.

"Good luck Mrs. McCandless," the sergeant said as they walked out of the barracks and into the cold. He picked up the hood.

*

Birchill: people still lived there, but there were many ghostly derelict houses, window-holes and doorways haphazardly boarded up, in these slum terraces.

The streetlights had all been stoned-out.

It was dark and scary, very scary to do this on her own, but Frankie and her had fallen out. He always wanted to do things his own way: "I'm off to do this right."

"That's right, Frankenstein. You run off and sulk," had been her last words to him.

So, alone, she decided to search them one by one, by herself. "Mum?" she called out again and again.

Natalie would learn some fifteen years later from a clairvoyant known locally as the Morrigan that the terraced house in Birchill Grove; a two storey hovel that she'd been able to walk right into: it was probably the one. The beyond-the-grave knowledge of that. For nights after, horrible dreams of that empty house haunted her awake; the doorway was up the drive, a side entry, it'd been cleared of planks— "Mary McCandless?"—no answer, always no answer—and she'd cry herself back to sleep. *She'd been too late. If only she'd been earlier, gone out to search the hour before.* The Morrigan confirmed this: by ten-thirty the interrogation would have been finished, and the I.R.A. would have taken her Mum away.

17

Under a pinched upper eyelid, the black hole of her pupil, which had been fixed and dilated, shrinking, reacting to the light. A sign that she was coming to. He let go of the eyelashes; the flesh slid back down the brown iris.

A last puff of the ciggy, snorting the smoke out his nostrils.

He stubbed the butt out on the concrete floor. He picked up the Colt .45. There were no two ways about it: if she was going to make it he'd have to get her to a hospital. They'd have to drive the V.W. Camper up to the entrance of Casualty, dump her out, and drive off like the hammers of Hell.

(Then he remembered—the other eight had taken the camper away to burn it out. They would have to do it in the back-up car, the Cortina.)

"We'll have to take her to the Royal," he said to the others, and stood up, knees all cramped-cold.

"Have you gone totally mental?" Bobby asked.

Gun in hand, muzzle pointed at the floor: "Look. She needs medical attention now or that's it."

"Then that's it." Bobby folded his spider-web-tattooed arms in disgust. The man was always pushing it, a big mouth, no skin on his face, relying on his family's heavyweight connections.

He checked the safety catch was on. "Do you want to meet the Unknowns Bobby? Or how's about a rep' as 'the Lady-killer' following you around the rest of your days, 'cause I don't fancy either of those options myself?"

"She's an informer, we execute informers," Bobby said with a shrug. "So what."

"So…" He just sighed and slid the Colt down into the back of his jeans.

Bobby's arms unfolded, two index fingers pointing at him. "The Royal—through all the patrols, no fucking way!"

He went over to where she was lying, intent on picking her up and leading by example. "I'm not going to argue about this. We're going. That's just the way it is, right."

*

(The so-called 'Unknowns' were rumoured to be the newly set up internal security units of the Provos. Staffed with faceless men, the Big Lad's enforcers, no criminal records, the terrorists of the terrorists. Their unspoken policy: to kill anyone, anyone at all, who was a threat to the Movement. There was no doubt in Donal's mind—he wanted to be an Unknown.)

18

The Car Bomb.

Frankie gave up his search of the Birchill area after a failed twenty minutes. He was raging. It was Natalie's idea, a stupid girly idea. Just like it was her idea to wait for two hours before going out to search for their Mum—"in case she comes back". She wasn't the boss. He knew where to go. It was no secret. He knew where the local Provos hung out, boozing till all hours in their side-street shebeen, the Car Bomb.

(This place got its grim name-tag after Bloody Friday, Friday 14th April 1972, when the Provos used their latest weapon against the Ulster statelet, detonating twenty-two bombs, ten of them car-bombs, all over the North, killing nine people. The details of the dead—that two were bomb-disposal soldiers, one was a teenaged boy, two were women, and four were working men. The number of wounded—a total of one hundred and twenty.)

Frankie knew what had to be done. He marched up Hangingtree Road like he thought his Dad would have, or better still, like an I.R.A. man in the honour guard of a Milltown funeral, swinging his arms high. He turned down Shaw Street, *wee buns*. He saw a car parked at the bottom of the street, engine on, lights off. Paying it no mind, he went and knocked on the steel door of the shebeen, a firm rapping.

An eye-slat racked back. "Yeah?"

"Where's my Mum?"

"Fuck away off kid." The eye-slat slammed closed.

He kicked the door. "Youse lot took my Mum tonight. Where is she?" He kicked it again.

The door swung open. The big blubbery doorman grabbed him by the arm and when he had a grip, cuffed him around the head. "What do you think you're doing?"

"Get off me. I'm here to find my Mum."

"There's no women in there so piss off." The doorman pushed him away.

"Youse took her! Her name is Mary McCandless."

That name. Inside the den it struck fear, drawing another shadowy figure out and into the night. "What's going on here Liam?"

The doorman made a joke of it: "This kid is looking for his mammy Joe."

"What's your name son?" The word 'son' was slurred on the 's'.

"Frankie."

"Come on in Frankie and have a drink with me."

He caught sight of the man's narrow old face in the moonlight. Sunken eyes. Long nose. A smile, thin-lips, all grey teeth. He was suddenly wary. This friendliness was not what he'd expected, not at all, and yet, why not, he hadn't done anything wrong...

(Even if, as he suspected, she, his Mum, had.)

"Come on. What's yours—a Guinness?"

Liam the doorman laughed, jowls jiggling, nervous round the Big Lad's right hand man and rightly so.

He decided to brave it out, *take it to the limit*, the whole nine yards.

"I'd take a Guinness."

"Right you would. But a Coke'll do, yeah?"

The old man took him past a sighing Liam and into the Car Bomb. He tramped through waves of sawdust on the floor, couldn't see much inside. It was dead dark so it was, the walls were black as stout, there wasn't a window unboarded in defence. And it was smoky, the wall lights trapped in a fagged-out fog...

There were two men, an empty stool and a constantly topped-up pint of Guinness waiting for the old man back at the bar.

A dismissal: "Bye lads. Talk to Fergus Rafferty down Newry way about the package. He's your man."

The men—it struck Frankie that the one on the left looked very like, *it couldn't be could it?* George Harrison—both said at once, a Beatles' harmony: "Cheers Joe."

He stood gawping at the Beatle who avoided his gaze like the plague. *No. Come on like, what would he be doing here?*

In the dimness, the old man held up a veined hand. "A Coke and a packet of crisps for the lad."

The men strode past Frankie, heading for the door. In profile: *No, it definitely isn't him.*

"I'm here to get my Mum back home," Frankie said to the old man.

The barman poured the order of Coke, fizzing.

"Do you know about it, where they took her?"

"No, but I'll find out for you, how's that?" The man slurred the 's' into a 'z' again.

"When?"

"Tomorrow. She'll likely be back by then though, won't she?"

The barman handed him his Coke and crisps.

"Give us one of those crisps, would you son?" said Joe.

95

Frankie let the man delve into his packet, *crackle-scrunch*, lifting out a handful of crushed crisps.

19

When I get back I will tell Natalie what a good girl she is, what a mother she will make, and Frankie how brave he was for defying the I.R.A., and Martin, how proud I am of him, if not his politics, how he holds up in Long Kesh I will never know, and I will hug Eddie to me and I will never let him go again and I'll read him his favourite bedtime story over and over till sleep comes, like I used to, The Billy Goat's Gruff, that old troll saying, Who's that clip-clopping across my bridge...clip-clopping...my bridge...Her eyes must have flicked open then because—

As he pulled her up, she was suddenly able to see him. All sentimentality banished at a glance. Flicker of his face. Devil with a human face, the black mask gone. Blink. He was young, a young man, cruel turn to his mouth, violent eyes; marked by utter ruthlessness as only a young man can be. Blink. And yet, his face, fuzzing in and out of focus, strangely handsome, if not good-looking. Familiar. *Who, who did he look like?* Holding her by the arms, drawing her up to him as in a dance, yes, he looked like her Frankie's pop idol, George Harrison, the Beatle. In front of her. Teenage girls screaming their lungs out. Her eyelids closed again, heavy.

(This pin-up was of course Donal.)

*

In an atherosclerosis (or chronically damaged vessel wall) in her thigh, due to a combination of a varicose vein and a baton injury sustained in the previous interrogation, a thrombus had been forming of platelets and the protein fibrinogen clipped to fibrin, plugging, more platelets, haemostasis (blood-standing), clumping, until it fully blocked the flow of blood in the vein. With the pumping of the restarted heart, and the surge of blood, a spiral section of it broke loose. The shocked and drastically weakened body reacted to this, a chemical message sent to secrete anti-coagulants system-wide, but it came too late.

20

Donal bent down, picked her up, and flopped her body over his shoulder. A fireman's lift.

"Mark my words," Bobby said to the others, "This is suicide-stupid."

She was very light. He carried her body out of the room with ease. Through the shadowy hall, into the ghostly light of the moon.

The others followed, slowly. He couldn't hear what they were saying but he could tell they were arguing, pros and cons, amongst themselves. *Let them.* Bobby would be emphasising the fact that although he didn't have the rank his mother's Uncle Pete was high-up and the whole family were involved, and to fuck with him was to…*What an arsehole!*

He checked to see the street was clear of folk—you could never be too careful, the Brits had old dolls and single mums and even schoolgirls spying for them these days—then he walked quickly three doors down the footpath to the car.

It was a dark blue Ford Cortina Dec' had nicked earlier that night from the Markets.

He clicked open the rear door and gently folded and moulded her into the back seat. He closed the door, quietly.

The others walked up.

"Who's coming with me?" he said, making it seem like there was a brave choice to make.

"I am." Dec' volunteered to drive.

"Me too," said Jim, more subdued.

"That's enough of us then," he said, cutting through anything Bobby might have to say. "Five in the car would look sus'."

"What?" said Bobby, his face bright and twisted terrible in the moon-glow.

"You heard me Bobby. Enjoy your walk home." He walked round to the driver-side rear, leaving Bobby just glaring at him, reddening. He got into the seat, closed the door.

Dec' went round and took the driving seat.

Jim got into the front, to ride shotgun.

Bobby banged on the windscreen: "You'll regret this Donal!"

Yeah, yeah, yeah. He'd heard and had a lot of threats in and to his life. Maybe he would regret this, but he knew he'd regret her dying on him a lot more.

Bobby raging: "I'll get you."

"Let's go," he said to Dec'.

Dec' started the car, pulled away from the curb, drove straight down the street.

Nobody looked back.

Check pulse—still there.

21

Special types of counter-insurgency techniques as practised by the British Army in Northern Ireland, part of the United Kingdom, in 1972, with the full approval of Faulkner's Stormont and tacit consent from Her Majesty's Government:

The infamous Helicopter Run. Practised on internees taken to Girdwood Barracks. Removed from the other prisoners. *Where are they taking you—and what for?* Blindfolded and barefoot and beaten with the butts of machine guns and batons. Guard dogs snapping at mud-crusted heels. Deafened by the roar and rotor-whine of a Wessex helicopter. Blasted, hair-whipping, by the downdraft. "Say your prayers you Fenian bastards! No more than you deserve." On the way to the hovering helicopter. "It's a long way down!" In the Wessex. "Tell us the names of everyone you know in the Provos, or else." Lift off. You have the tremendous sensation of rising, soaring up to a terrifying altitude. "Talk or we'll shove you out." No reply. Travelling up the spine tremors of terror. Pushed out of the helicopter. Screaming, half a scream, cut off, hitting the ground on your back. A drop of only four feet. Next prisoner. Function of technique: show of strength, terrorisation of enemy, a morale -destroying revenge. This is the Army, sniper-shit-scared, letting off steam.

The White Noise Room, Palace Barracks: Hooded dark

(hooding produces disorientation and hallucinations). Ordered to stand—*where, where do you want me to stand, I can't see anything*—with feet apart. A loud high-pitched hissing mushing machine-like noise from somewhere—the 'buzz-saw'. Forced to lean forwards, up against a wall. Fingertips to the wall. Only the fingertips. A punch in the ribs. "Hold that position" (the classic Soviet 'Stoika' or wall-standing speciality). "If you move from that position one inch you will be for it you cunt." Fingers, under pressure, become painful, excruciatingly so, then wrists, elbows, shoulders, until every joint, every sinew and muscle, is screaming for you to move. The droning of that static, monotonous sound smothers the winces, small grunts of pain you make. Agony passes and a heavy numbness settles in; the weight of your body feels unbearable. "Cry out and we will kick seven bells out of you." Try up to forty-three of hours of this on and off mixed with periods of complete immobilisation. Aim of technique: Sensory Deprivation. To distort normal body metabolism and brain function by restricting the flow of blood nutrients to the brain and deprive it of the stimulation that the mind requires. Extremely effective in rendering subjects suggestible (and confessional) when used in conjunction with sleep deprivation, starvation, and tactile deprivation (being forced to wear overalls that are several sizes too big). *Requiring detainees to stand with their arms against a wall* but not in a position of stress *provides security for detainees and guards against physical violence.* (The Compton Whitewash, 1971.)

Severe beating of the detainee's genital region: Gough Barracks, Armagh. You are sometimes stripped, sometimes not, as interrogators, trained to leave as few marks on the body for the medical record, hold you down and concentrate their blows and kicks on one sensitive (nerve-rich) area, specifically the penis and testicles of the male. Aim: it can only be cruelty.

Gun to the head: R.U.C. Castlereagh Holding Centre: a loaded gun is placed to your head. "Tell us everything now or we'll kill you, dump your body in a sheugh and put the word out that the Loyalists got you." Aim of this technique: Counter-terrorism information.

Cigarette burning (widespread usage by vengeful sniper-scared squaddies all over Ulster): A lit ciggy is applied to the surface of the skin in particularly visible areas. Aim: disfiguration, brutalisation of the minority population—torture used to shut people up not get them to talk.

Threats to family and friends: a psychological torture. Man is by nature a social animal, a political animal (if not necessarily a moral animal). Informing internees/detainees/political prisoners that their loved ones, their children, had been attacked by Loyalists or the Army while they were unable to defend them was a sadistic way of increasing their distress.

The process of interrogation (under emergency powers legislation): hours and hours of repetitive questioning, usually punctuated by verbal abuse, threats, and physical beatings. Perfected into a blunt art by the R.U.C. Special Branch, the S.A.S., 14th Intelligence Unit. Aim: evidence collection, breaking the 'interrogatee', potentially turning the source against their former comrades.

*

(All these tortures were practised indiscriminately on mainly Catholic civilians. Only a small percentage of the victims were serving I.R.A. Volunteers due to the fact that most senior officers had been informed of internment well in advance of its implementation and had retreated to the sanctuary of the Irish Republic to ride out the storm.)

22

A sightless murk, this darkness. She was aware of thrumming though. An engine? The sensations of being driven, vaguely cradled in a seat. She tried to see if she could see, anything? Consciousness—her eyes slid open once more, carefully mind, narrowly barely under control. The slit-world beyond the watery wooze in her head, a gnawing weariness and weight at her temples. Tears escaping. She saw the two men in the front seats. A dim peripheral vision of a man to her right. Back to the front: she saw the road ahead, it was wide, the broken centre line slewing right corner, the tarmac pool-lit by the streetlights. She saw a traffic light in the distance: flick green to orange.

That's it! The red light.

She was weeping but this was her opportunity to get away. Escape them again. This time, forever.

The car braked, gears grinding down to a halt.

She would wait till all the fitful forward momentum had passed and the vehicle had stopped dead. Then she would grab the handle, rip the door open and run, screaming, run, hands in the air...

*

Desperation: this was how she had escaped the night before, the night of the 6th—

Hooded silence. The questions about where she'd been that summer, about the Army, about who her handler was… It had been quiet for a long time in the black.

Nothing?

"Is anyone there? Let me go! Is anyone there?"

The only sounds: her breathing, laboured, her heart, flitting, stammering, banging in her chest, a gargantuan gulp of a swallow.

I can't believe it. Have they gone?

Left me.

Have you left me—truly? Oh God, yes.

Struggling to get free, an instinctual frenzy. Rocking the chair, side to side, she was tied to, side to side.

"Help. Help me please somebody!"

Rocking the chair, until it and she veered off to the left and crunched down into the floor splintering cracking and a winding blast of pain in her side.

The ropes were suddenly loose, her arms her own again.

On her knees, her hands went for the hood, wrenching it off. It was dim-dark in the room. No lights. Only the faint bluing of the moon leaking in through the half boarded-up window. She felt around her face, wincing, it was puffed swollen round her eyes nose and mouth. *But I am alive.*

And I am free.

I am free…

She pushed herself up from her stocking knees to her stocking feet.

Moonbeams cutting across her rising form. She looked down at her body in the paling moonlight. Her arms were bruised. Her blouse was ripped. Her skirt, all dirtied. She had no shoes, her good heels. No coat. No handbag. *No money to get home?*

And there was this rip, a leg-long ladder in her support-tights, the thick-webbed ones she had to wear to help with the thrombosis. That was when all rationality left her and she started screaming, inhuman wailing, hysterical flight out of the house and into the benighted streets of Belfast, the hood clamped into her hand.

This was how the sergeant of the Scots Guards was to find her.

23

The spiralling thrombus is pumped *boom-boom*, at a highly stressed heart-rate of one hundred and fifty beats per minute, all the way up her inferior vena cava, *boom-boom*, quickly through all the counter-gravity valves until it catches in one of these back-flow stop-flaps and is briefly halted. Soon though, it will be entering the right atrium of her heart. From here it will descend through the tricuspid valve and into the right ventricle. Milliseconds after, when the right ventricle contracts, *boom-boom*, it will squeeze the de-oxygenated blood and the clot into one of the two pulmonary arteries. These highly pressurised vessels connect the heart to the narrowing network of capillaries that line the lungs. (Some capillaries around the alveoli are so narrow that only one red blood cell can pass through them at one time.) It is here that a clot the size of this one can cause a critical circulatory blockage, *boom-boom, boom-boom*, a pulmonary embolism. If that happens the partially malfunctioning lung will not oxygenate the blood, the pressurised blood will back up to the heart, the heart will starve of oxygen as it struggles on, the brain too, and she will die—like this.

*

But Virgo is supposed to be the astrological House of Health. This is what superstitious Natalie would tell her. Her poor daughter-turned-mother, who like many children of that time had not attended school regularly and was way behind in her Maths, English, History, Geography, Sciences, had read a library book on astrology. She knew that Hermes, walker between worlds, bearing his caduceus (the very symbol of Western medicine, two snakes coiling around a sword), is the ruler of this House of the zodiac. *Don't worry. It's in the stars, the very heavens themselves, they'll get you to the hospital, you'll be all right Mum.*

*

The clot is pumped free of the clinging valve. When your health fails it is the role of Hermes to deliver you to the afterlife.

24

Headlights up ahead on the road. A man in a dark oncoming car will brake slow and stop for her and seeing that she is being pursued he will allow her to get in, all bloodied and battered, but he will have to reverse back down the way he came if they are to get away because the Provos are running after them and one of them, shouting, yelling, ordering, has a gun pointing at the car. Revs, stick-shift, the high whine of reverse gear and the startled cry of the man "Hey!" as the front windscreen is *smack*-holed, the back-windscreen too, *whizz*, a bullet clean-through, with no one's name on it. Swerving into a U-turn her getaway car will be gunned and accelerate away from danger, leaving the torturers behind somewhere in the darkness. "Are you all right?" She did not answer the man. *The Good Samaritan. The Good Samaritan.* "We better get you to a hospital love." Headlights in her eyes, blinding light.

25

"—Seriously though Donal, what with everybody in the Brigade who is anybody being slung into Long Kesh, or banged up down South, there's no reason that you can't rise through the ranks quick-smart."

And though he'd been chuffed with this statement of his potential, to be patted on the head by someone so senior as Joe, so respected in the Movement, buying him a pint, paying him mind, quickly, and a little too curtly, he said, "I hope that isn't the only reason I'd be promoted Joe?"

Standing beside him at the bar, the old man considered this remark, thoughtfully, the way he seemed to weigh up all that was said to him. He nodded, and smiled. Words chosen strategically:

"You're a very capable man Donal. An ambitious man. Anyone can see that. I think you'd make a fine counter-intelligence officer. Let's see how you go with this McCandless situation tomorrow night..."

*

A sudden hacking, a seizure of breath and she was spasming violently, wriggling, squirming in the back seat, then her body went rigid.

It took him totally by surprise. "Christ, no!"

He felt her neck for a carotid pulse.

All over the place, wild erratic.

Jim: "What's wrong?"

She was spasming again, hands flapping, feet kicking. A choking noise, like a rattle in her throat. And her body sagged loose.

Dec' looked back. "Do you want me to stop?"

"Not in here. Not in here?" He couldn't do C.P.R. properly in a car, the seats, there wasn't enough room.

Check pulse—Gone.

Her eyes blank, staring at nothing.

He grabbed her hair and pulled her lolling head over. "Mary!" he shouted spit into her face.

Jim: "Can't you do that C.P.-thingy-ma-jig on her again?"

That's when he saw there was fresh dark red blood on her lips. *She'd coughed up blood. That meant internal injuries!* And he didn't know what else he could do. *He hadn't hit her hard enough in the body for internal injuries, had he?*

A film of blood darkening her teeth. He'd tried everything he knew. *You bitch you—what else can I do?*

*

As the clot clogged the entrance to her lungs—and blood, an overflow rising slick to her throat, choking on it, the thick coppery ore, gargle, a last rasp, a red red mist expelled into the car—she died.

26

Except: under piercing lights suddenly she was being wheeled in on a stretcher strapped flat on her back with an oxygen mask on her ashen face, a line in, amid intense surgical light and unfamiliar faces, that harsh reek of hospital chlorine, the scrutiny of medical eyes, *I'm alive*, in a matter of seconds she was lifted onto a table and being examined in the Accident and Emergency Department of the Royal (she should know she'd been there often enough) for a P.E. whatever a P.E. was, but the team of them, these white-coated strangers did not seem to be holding out much hope for her the dying mother—"How long has she been down?"—yet they carried on trying all they knew how to try to resuscitate her. No pulse. E.C.G.: nil. No breathing. No name—"Do we have a name?" *My name is Mary McCandless. Flat 42, Donard Flats.* "No means of identification, I see?" They proceeded to slice open her chest *please don't hurt me* between the breasts, exposing the blood-starved muscle there and the ribs below, a rib-cracker applied explosive jerk of the arms and *snap!* the sternum broken, the ribs pushed back like wings, they were into her chest cavity. "Got to get more blood into her." A tracing of the clot to her left pulmonary artery. Scalpel. Incision into the artery wall. Retrieval of the thrombus. Checking for other clots. Suction, mopping up. Suturing the vessel wound, rapid precise stitches. Metal tongs curled yellow wires direct electro-stimulation of the heart. No response. Higher voltage. Reapplication of the tongs. Smoke-reek of burning flesh. *Boom-boom.* E.C.G. wave. Flatline. Charging. "Go again!" *Boom-boom.* The heart's pumping restored, the lungs began to function to suck in the pure oxygen from the mask, *boom-boom* the blood began to flow, a flush rush push of life into the corpse and the dying mother was resurrected: *I am the resurrection and the light. He who believeth in me, though he die, he shalt not perish.*

*

CAUTION: Hold on if you must, but in the end you will come to me, the love of your life.

27

"She's dead," Donal said, fingers slipping from her neck.

The sudden hot reek of ammonia, *aw Jesus Christ*, she'd pissed herself. Loss of bladder control, confirmation: "She's tatty-fucking bread!"

"Uniting Ireland's not worth shedding blood for," big brother Oisin told him over a pint of Harp, "Are you really willing to kill for a set of ideas?"

Dec' dabbed the brakes down to a stop and pulled the Cortina into the curb. "Where till?"

Windows frantically wound down. The stink.

Jim: "Yeah, what the fuck are we going to do with her now?"

He'd grabbed Oisin by the scruff of his scrawny studenty neck, a hissed prophecy of spit in his brother's pasty face: "Listen you patronising wanker. I'll kill for freedom if it comes to it. While you sit picking morals out of your arse down South."

"Donal," said Dec' over his shoulder, eyes locked on the road. "Tell us where we're going will you?"

He and Oisin left the Crown Liquor Saloon after that; they went their separate ways; ways which had not met since.

Well, there was no two ways about it now. It was done. *The stupid bitch had done it for him.* He'd killed, albeit accidentally, for Ireland and now he'd have to tell Joe, to come clean, and if he could—to call in the marker. *Joe would see him right?*

"The Car Bomb," he said. The car stank of her. "Head for the Car Bomb Dec'."

Dec' took off.

Oisin took after his Da, John Keenan Bookmakers Ltd. 'The Betting Man' wouldn't lift a trigger finger to help the Movement either. Too much to lose. Three shops. One in the city centre. An irreligious if superstitious clientele of masochistic gamblers, none too fussy about whose pockets they lined on the way to that big, big win.

He himself took after his Ma's brother, Tyrone-born Brendan Cairns, a legendary hero of the Flying Columns that characterised the late fifties campaign; captured by Irish Special Branch and interned by the Irish Republic in the Curragh in 1958; close personal enemy of Cathal Goulding and his dogma of anti-physical-force republicanism. "Brits out, that's all the Cause's about son!" A slogan, a pat on the head, tousled hair, a hearty laugh. He only met the fire-headed bulk of a man at the bar of The Irish Whip when they went to Sligo to get away from the Twelfth, but his mother never stopped talking about Uncle Brendy's brave exploits—long after the blazing row when his sell-out of a father told her to quit it, that she was making up fairy tales, adding that Brendan, the drunken renegade he was, would have fought his own shadow and had been booted out for not obeying a direct order. His Ma was insistent in private: her Brendan resigned in defence of his sense of personal honour, the higher moral ground.

Jim: "We're going to see the Joe, right?"

Nerve-jitters in the bitch's hands, flapping, grabbing, on the seat like she was still alive.

"Aye," he said.

118

28

THE FOLLOWING IS AN EXTRACT FROM A PRESS
RELEASE BY THE S.D.L.P. PRINTED IN *THE IRISH
SPECTATOR* 19th JANUARY 1973:

*Clearly, we need to determine the whereabouts of Mrs. Mary
McCandless, but at present the level of publicity this case is generating is
counter-productive. Mrs. McCandless is likely afraid that reporters will
find out where she is hiding. Undoubtedly, the publicity was useful in the
first place. It has elicited widespread condemnation of the horrific way
this poor woman has been treated and it has turned people against the
people responsible for driving her away. But the publicity should be eased
off if it is preventing her from returning to her family. We do not believe
Mrs. Mary McCandless is being held captive. We have appealed to
those involved that she should be allowed to come home without further
threat of violence. Assurances have been given. We don't believe there is
anything else that can be done but wait for her to come back of her own
accord.*

*

A young man knocking at the front door of Flat 42, he
looked vaguely familiar, *skinny fella, from up Andersonstown way,*

119

what's his name? "Are you Natalie McCandless?" he asked.

"Yes, who are you?" she said.

Her mother's missing purse handed over. "Here. Take it."

Soft leather on her palms, a caress. "How did you... Where did you get this?"

It was the third of January; for nearly a month now she'd been waiting for her Mum to come home, for word a sign, anything, climbing the walls.

Jim shrugged. "I was told to give it to you. That's all I know." (It was Donal who'd given him the purse and told him to do the delivery—because his face wasn't so well-known in the area.)

She opened the catch. Hand delving into the lining. Money. Ten quid, the right amount, *she'd been carrying a tenner that night, I know, I saw because she gave me her change for the fish suppers.* And God, a handful of rings—

One-diamond, a gold ring, declaring her engagement.

The Claddagh, two hands grasping at a crowned heart, her wedding ring.

And the eternity ring, three diamonds on this never-ending circle, symbolising her father's undying love.

Why are they giving me back her rings? What does this mean—oh God, please no! I don't believe it. I won't believe it. She looked up, sudden anger. The man had started to walk away.

She ran after him, grabbed a hold of the sleeve of his jacket, tugged at it. "Where's my Mum, please tell me?"

"Look, get off me, I told you, I don't know." Jim ripped his arm free and held her off.

"What have you done with her? I'm begging you. Tell us please," Natalie said, tears clouding her eyes, but the man started to walk faster and she dropped one of the rings—

Eternity. Rolling, a faint tinkling, away towards the gutter.

She ran after it, trapped it with her foot before it went into a grate. She bent down to pick it up, diamond-flash, slipping it on her ring finger, a perfect fit. *She would not believe it.*

She looked up. But—

The man was gone, disappeared altogether—*probably ducked down the stairs?*

She snapped the purse shut, and ran to the stairwell.

A threat yelled out: "I know who you are, you bastard!"

But there was no one down there. Not a single soul.

And her threat was reduced to a mocking echo, thrown back at her by the narrow void.

29

In the hospital, another hospital, a mental hospital. The E.C.T. Suite. Pre-medicated, sedated to a dizzy daze. "I don't want to do this today." Nurses guiding her, the chronically depressed patient, held under Section Twelve of the Mental Health Act, not letting her retreat from the psychiatrist. "Now, now, it's for your own good Mary, you know that." Her body being strapped to the electric bed. "But I don't want to, please, no." *I have been sent back to take care of my children.* Muscle relaxant. Injected in the bound-down left arm. Paralysis. *Can't move. Can't budge. Can't speak. Can't protest.* Fearful if drugged eyes open to see electrodes primed, the body made ready. The familiar hum of voltage. Fasted since midnight so she would not be sick in the therapy session. Injection of general anaesthetic. "Look at my eyes Mary. Good. One, two, three…" *I am…* Blackness… Then altogether gone in a flash of blessed light.

*

Ruthie Ruthie Ruthie: screaming, then suddenly still, lifeless, a doll after the fall. Unconscious. A rush to intensive care. *How did this happen Mrs. McCandless?* The wee skull fractured,

123

brain injuries near fatal to cerebral hemispheres, the thinking and life support centres, coma. Her distraction, her negligence near infanticide, or was it? Harold, head in his hands in the waiting room. *How could you let this happen? You are such a terrible mother. You need to be punished.* Unspoken accusations, allegations. The R.U.C. would arrest her, surely? She was not fit to be... But no, when Ruthie came out of coma in a week and through a protracted recovery period of three months, they entrusted Ruthie to her care once more. She was almost afraid to touch her baby, her baby girl again. It was Harold who carried her home, and cradled and bottle-fed her for the first few days. She could only look on, a bystander uttering prayers for strength. Ruthie was quiet, so still, so tiny in her Daddy's arms. Not a peep out of her. And when she did dare to get Ruthie to breast-feed, the tiny little lips would not take the nipple. Was this was the same bouncing baby who'd screamed her lungs out if she didn't get as much milk from her breast as she wanted?

"You're going to have to do it," her Mum June told her. "You can't take care of her yourself anymore, not with the two others bairns to look after." Ruthie was four. And unable to learn, to speak, to walk, to feed herself. The poor child had grown though—physically, but her body was all skin and bones, wasted. They wanted to put the poor child in a home, "for her own good". Unable to dress herself, go to the toilet, to smile, to laugh, to do much more than recognise you sometimes with her eyes. 'They' being the nurses, her Mum, her father, and Harold who she had not been able to make love to since, have sex with yes, but not give herself over fully to. "Ruthie has special needs darling. We, you, can't be there for her all the time. The nurses can." *If I had been there all the time, or even just that one time, she wouldn't be like this...* She wondered if precious wee Martin could speak, and newborn Natalie, would they say to shove their weak sister out of the nest—to fall down, down…

It was the impact with pram wheel that caused the intracerebral haematoma—a brain bleed. And the blood built up in the skull, too much swelling in so small a head, intense pressure on the delicate tissues. "Falls of this nature, even up to four feet, are rarely this damaging," the Intensive Care paediatrician had said, sympathetically, so long ago. "Very unfortunate." *But I know what I have done.*

The hospital minibus brought Ruthie back every weekend. That was the deal. She would take her first-born back every weekend and look after her, "like I should be doing", let the family look after her, their own, "like we all should be doing". Ruthie would sit there in her wheelchair, spastic twitches at the dinner table, and she'd sit next to her and feed her the mushed-up food like a baby. And this, when "Rag doll Ruthie" (her biggest best boy Martin's nickname for his elder sister) was the age of ten.

*

I don't want to live anymore: a cry for help?

Therapy Session One: The silver-haired consultant psychiatrist sitting behind his desk, staring over a pile of files intently at her. He has a speech he gives to all his new suicidal depressed patients but, as he has partaken of a delicious lunch with an old boyhood chum-cum-Judge at The Reform Club, and more importantly, read her case file, he decides to do this off the cuff so to speak: "The human conscious mind is perhaps the only entity on the planet, and perhaps in the Universe, that has the capacity to abstract and conceptualise the future. The need for a positive sense of the future is one of the prime motivators of human life. This need transcends death. We do not want to think death is the end. Heaven, a life after death with God and lost loved ones, fulfils this need for religious persons like yourself Mrs. McCandless. In the normal scheme of things, this should help you get by—statistically those with religious beliefs do not get depressed as often as say, atheists, yes? Unfortunately, you, or at least part of your psyche, have developed a dangerous death fantasy centred around your afterlife belief in which it is more appealing to be there than here with your children. This aberration is what we have to deal with, see in a different light, if we are to help you come to terms with your life as it stands at present. Yes?" (Tremors.) "Good. Now, tell me how you're feeling on the lithium—is it helping to stabilise your mood-swings?" "Yes?" (Tremors are a side effect of 800mg daily dose of Lithium Carbonate they had her on.) "Good, good."

*

Suicide is not the quick-fix to your problem that it may seem. Suicide is an end before a solution can be found. Suicide leaves your problem behind for those you love to deal with. These are the sort of 'thought-corrections' she would write in her tremor-filled letters to her mother June, who it seems did not want to visit her in this place…

(She would not find out till after her release that her sixty-two-year-old mother had in fact been hospitalised, with a broken hip, by the U.V.F. for refusing to contribute to the Force's funds—"Pay you lot after what you did to my Mary, no way!")

30

"That tout. She's away off whoring in East Belfast they say. Shacked up with a U.D.A. battalion commander. Up the duff already. Couldn't give a toss about her old family, hadn't even bothered to contact them. It's not a bit of wonder she was given a good hiding, or that she isn't showing her face round here again."

(This was Mary's afterlife, the life not lived. And how could it be?—it was an I.R.A. lie like the version where she ran off with a soldier-boy. The proof: Mary had had a hysterectomy so how could she have another child, or family with anyone else?)

It was a story invented for her by the rumour-mongering of the woman who did not wear a mask in the abduction—the one with the beady blue eyes. She was very pleased to have been instructed to carry out a disinformation campaign by *Cumann na mBan*. To destroy the remains of Mary's name, her very memory, the image of her in her own childrens' minds, was a pleasure for her. Why?—because it was part of a family feud. Her name was Moira Ward, second eldest daughter of the notorious Republican Ward clan. And it had been her who'd first brought the name of Mary McCandless to the local Provos' attention when Mary had refused to pay her mother the agreed price for a three-piece suite. "What the fuck is she doing living here anyway?" Moira was keen to put on record. "Fucking wee tea-leaf. She's lucky we don't treat her the way her kind treat us."

*

Natalie, now Natalie Kelly, a wife and mother of five herself, can recall her mum taking delivery of the blue, cigarette-burned, three-piece suite a fortnight after coming out of the psychiatric ward of Purdysburn Hospital. Mary had paid a fair price. It was the Wards' demands for more after the incident with the soldier:

—spreading rumours about her being a Brit-loving informer, proof of the pudding, she's not involved in the Chain—

—bad-mouthing Martin for being a fucking Stickie—

—threatening her that if she didn't pay, a back-street settlement would be enforced—

that made her mum Mary dig her heels in and tell them to take their bloody suite back and give her the money. The Wards did not take the suite back. Somebody, namely Moira, let it be known that Mary was an Army spotter with a transmitter in her place.

*

European Convention on Human Rights: Article Nine: Section 1: Everyone has the right to freedom of thought, conscience and religion; this includes freedom to change his religion or belief, and freedom, either alone or in a community with others and in public or private, to manifest his religion or belief, in worship, teaching, practise and observance.

31

Wait: I cannot die now! I was sent back. My son needs me. She was supposed to visit Martin tomorrow, wasn't she? Every Thursday like clockwork she got on the local relief committee's minibus out of West Belfast, up the M1 to Lisburn and Long Kesh.

This is how she met Christina. Her son Ger was interned too, since April. They would sit together and wait in the bus at the gates, to get in to the car park. Christina talked. She listened (words were hard to string together after Harold's passing, she became withdrawn).

"My Ger is innocent, has never been in the Provos or the Stickies. He's a Peoples' Democracy man, a socialist.

"N.I.C.R.A. (Northern Ireland Civil Rights Association) are organising a march in the city centre next Monday. Will you come with me? Ah, come on, you have to get out more, get involved, it's all political now. There's nothing wrong with peaceful protest.

"My Ger was framed. Did you know the Special Branch man told him he was going to be in for three months minimum because when he was picked up he was carrying a copy of *The United Irishman*. Three months. When they allow it in the prison every week. Not that those bastards had to tell him what the reason was at all…"

(Martin was innocent, just because he hung around with

Stickies didn't mean he was one. She'd known for a long time—since '69 when they'd been forced out and he'd turned fifteen—that he was hanging around with fellas in the Officials. Harold used to try to talk to the lad, but all he got back was Che Guevara and Communist ideology, the mass man and capitalism, uniting the working classes [Prods included because they were just deluded], the world revolution, the right to fight back, and there'd be blazing rows. One time Martin, commenting on his father's sol-diering, accused Harold of being at best an Imperialist dupe, at worst a Nazi: that provoked a fist-fight which, shrieking, she had to break up.)

Christina: "Did you know this was where they built those Stirling Bombers to re-supply the R.A.F. in World War Two—no, neither did I—Ger told me last time."

They would wait in the car park to have their permits—a piece of paper that had taken her four weeks to get, four weeks of worrying not being able to see Martin after they took him—individually verified by the screws (Martin's word).

(She'd baked him a chocolate birthday cake. Implanted seventeen candles on the iced top. All the family were waiting for his homecoming, when the news rushed in on the heels of a fourteen-year-old friend of Natalie's: "They've lifted him.")

She would get off the bus. A cup of the Quakers weak tea. Standing in a drafty, leaking old hut. On the edge, always kept on the edge because she wasn't one of theirs, not really. At first she'd tried to make polite conversation, ask political questions, feign interest, but the looks she got: loose tongues lose lives and all that.

All the women's talk, mothers' talk mainly, would be

routine, of the dreadful conditions in the camp and the poor boys, and how Commandant Truesdale was a fascist tyrant, the next public protest against Internment, and when all this madness was ever going to end. Another wait, lists of names being called out all the time, almost an hour.

The waiting was how they tortured the relatives. The waiting, and the not knowing when Martin would be released.

"Mrs. McCandless? Proceed to the prison minibus." "See you later Christina." "Good luck Mary. I hope it goes all right today." There would be that short drive into the old Shorts Brothers aerodrome turned prison compound, the driver none too careful with the brakes, anti his passengers all the way.

She would enter another smelly hut, rotten wood and sweat. There they would search her, a full body search, conducted by a stern old uniformed woman, pockets turned out, suspicious, intrusive. "Clean. Go on through Mrs. McCandless." Another screw, leading her into the waiting room, another hut, another half hour spell of waiting.

Sometimes she would bring a copy of *Good Housekeeping* to look at the pictures of rich peoples' houses, you couldn't read when you were waiting.

CAUTION: The light of death is coming my love. Let go, and I will show your soul everything you ever wanted to know.

There would be a call sometime and the correct procedure was—she would get up and meet the screw at the door and be accompanied by him, silently, through a walkway, barbed wire on either side. Into the cage, one of the many cages. Up into the Stalag-type hut. This was the Visitors' Room. Sixteen booths crammed full of missing and catching up under watchful eyes.

Half an hour to see her biggest best boy.

It would have broken Harold's heart to see his son sitting there, long-lank-haired, beard-fuzz, a prisoner of war.

"Hello son."

Martin would smile when he saw her, he always had a warm winning smile. The girls liked him. This was his youth, he should have been going out, dancing, laughing, drinking a little, maybe finding a job, putting some money away…

"I'm going on hunger strike Mum." And he would be so pleased with his martyred self as he would reel off their renewed list of demands for that coming week:

1. The right to attend religious services on Sunday
2. Visiting conditions improved
3. Prisoner welfare to be monitored by Ministry inspectors
4. Free association between the cages
5. A gym, physical training facility
6. Educational facilities, a library
7. An entertainment programme (bringing in bands from outside to perform in the prison)

She would not try not to cry. This long string of misery. She would not break down in front of him.

Instead, the collapse occurred in private. *I want this to end. No more waiting.* Those pills, tranquillisations lined up on the dining table: four rows of seven blue barbiturate dots. No one else around…

Except: for Natalie, home early from school, a premonition she would later claim. *I knew you were going to do something bad Mum, I just knew it…*

*

136

"I wasn't bad Mum, I wasn't." A giggle, a naked waddle up to her mummy who was wagging a finger at her. "Daddy wanted it doing."

Daddy, under a mound of Saharan sand, only his head poking out, a sand-encrusted smile to June.

Mummy laughing.

Mummy laughing more, as her eldest brother Malcolm jumped up on the mound, the king of Greencastle. "And you're the dirty rascal!" the boy told his wee sister.

You could see across the mouth of the Lough, clear as a sunny day, to the South, the South. She had never been to the South, and her Daddy said she wouldn't ever want to go because it was a bad place.

"I want to be buried next!" she told her Daddy and big brother Malcolm. "I want to be buried next."

"You're too small," Malcolm told her.

So little Virgo the Virgin started to cry, to wail as best a five-year-old can, but no one would bury her alive because when the lungs have stopped breathing, and the heart has stopped pumping, and the blood has stopped flowing, the brain dies, the mind simply is no more.

Disappeared Searches in Vain

Andrew O'Hagan,
The Irish Telegraph, (25th May 2000)

The Independent Commission for the Location of Victims remains has called off all operations to find the bodies of the missing six I.R.A. murder victims.

The Northern Ireland Commissioner, Michael Sloan, said, 'In spite of information received by the I.R.A. we have not been able to recover the bodies. Gardai at the sites have put in an effort way beyond the call of duty, but the digs could not continue indefinitely. It is disappointing that the victims' families have not been able to give them a decent Christian burial. Perhaps there is another way to bring some feeling of closure because it would be awful if these families were left grieving forever.'

The current round of excavations for the so-called 'disappeared' began on the 4th May and has run the scheduled three weeks without any further successes. Gardai were looking for remains of Mary McCandless at Churchtown Strand, Co. Louth; Columba McVeigh at Bragan in Co. Monaghan; Danny McIlhone at Ballynultagh, Co. Wicklow; Kevin McKee and Seamus Wright in Coghallstown near Navan in Co. Meath.

Last year Gardai recovered the bodies of Eamon Molloy hidden in a coffin in a Louth graveyard, and John McClory and Brian McKinney, whose remains were found in a peat bog after weeks of digging in County Monaghan.

Gardai Superintendent Joseph Twomey said 'I have been involved in the digs from the beginning. You would try not to get emotionally involved, but it was difficult. My heart goes out to the families at this time.'

Spokesperson for the 'Relatives of the Disappeared' action group and daughter of Mary McCandless, Natalie Kelly, said, 'We accept this because we have to accept it.

After thirty years we know they're dead, but their bodies are still out there, somewhere. We don't have graves to visit to remember them.

The law, this Northern Ireland Location of Victims Remains Bill they've set in stone, now protects these I.R.A. murderers from prosecution. But there is nothing to protect the innocent, the families.'

32

Dec' hit the brakes outside the Car Bomb.

Donal's orders to the driver: "Park aways down the street. You stay in the car…"

Dec' slammed his hand off the steering wheel. "—With this smell for company—cheers like."

"Any bother, take off," he said, ignoring the protest, "Lose them."

"And what if I can't?" Dec' asked.

"Abandon it somewhere, burn it, her in it," he replied. *Pray for all our sakes it doesn't come to that.*

Jim and he got out of the car.

Dec' took off down the street.

Looking after the car: flare of brake lights on brick walls. Red and blue light mingling. The blue, the moon glaring down, reflection of the sun, almost bright enough to light the night, but not quite.

Play it cool. Keep it cool. Think about how Uncle Brendy… No, on second thoughts, don't be thinking about Uncle Brendy. Except his honesty…Just be straight with Joe and he'll be straight with you. He walked up to the door of the shebeen and knocked the door.

The eye-slat racked back.

"Come on on in lads," said Liam the doorman.

The door swung open. He led the way into the darkness. "Joe in?" he asked.

141

"Aye, at the bar, where else?" replied Liam, flexing a roly-poly smile.

He walked up to the bar, mouth dry, tongue all tacky. *The meting out of back street justice. A good kicking. A kangaroo court martial. A double tap to follow.*

"Donal. How's it going?" said Joe, supping on his sleek pint of stout, looking pleased to see him.

"Not too hot Joe," he said and stepped in closer so he could lower his voice. "We have a wee problem."

"What is it?" said Joe.

He took a deep breath. "She's gone and died on us."

A hiss of Guinness. "She's what!"

"We weren't that hard on her. But—"

The old man's eyes were hard on him, looking into him, through him. "Fucking hell Donal!"

"I know. I know. That's why I came straight here."

"Where's the...you know?"

"In the car outside."

"Outside here?"

"Where else was I going to take it?"

A dreadful sigh. "I'll talk to you about that later. For now, just put a cork in it the pair of you and let me think, like."

Thinking—

While you're thinking—think of your brother Kevin.

Thinking—

Donal heard two bangs on the door outside. And Liam telling someone to fuck away off, *was it?*

The old man thought for a bit more, looking down into his pint, seeking a way out of the sticky situation.

Think Kevin and how I saved his bacon and how this is all going to look—me, your man, getting done for this?

There were the sound-snatches of the door of the Car

142

Bomb opening and Liam and someone going at it:

"Get off me…"

"Piss off…"

Words chosen carefully, like a dogma, Joe spoke. "Right well. There's no option. It has to be a bog job."

"A what?" asked Jim.

"The stiff has to vanish, and south of the border mind, for all our sakes," Joe said, "We can't have this turning into our fucking Ranger Best."

(Ranger William Best was a nineteen-year-old Catholic from the Creggan, home on leave from the Royal Irish Rangers, when the Official I.R.A. murdered him in cold blood. He had never served in Northern Ireland. Two hundred women from the Creggan and the Bogside marched to the Official Republican Headquarters in 'Free Derry' to protest at his killing. This, combined with the botched bombing of the Aldershot Barracks, in which five kitchen workers, all of them women, and a Catholic Army padre, were killed, led the Goulding leadership to declare their ceasefire [whilst reserving the right to defend Nationalist areas from Army or Loyalist attack].)

From the escalating conflict outside, a child's voice rang out, clear as day: "Youse took her! Her name is Mary McCandless."

"I'll deal with this," Joe told them, "Best I handle the Big Lad too so keep your gobs shut till I say so."

*

'The Big Lad' was second-in-command of the Belfast

Brigade. It was him who set up the Unknowns. The nickname had the ring of 'The Big Fella' Michael Collins about it, a fearful reverence. History revising itself.

33

Geneva Convention IV: Article 24: The Parties to the conflict shall take the necessary measures to ensure that children under fifteen, who are orphaned or are separated from their families as a result of war, are not left to their own resources, and that their maintenance, the exercise of their religion and their education are facilitated in all circumstances.

*

The I.R.A. left the McCandless children to their own resources. They ran those rings round to them, and that was it, apart from the worst part of thirty years of stigma and enforced silence.

Natalie was too frightened to alert anyone to their plight. Frankie's advice heeded: "Don't squeal and sit tight and they'll let her go." They lived off Mary's Army widow's pension, cashing it illegally at the post office, waiting for her mother to come home. *It won't be long now...*

The cooker had still not been connected coming up to Christmas. *She wouldn't miss Christmas with us, would she?*

The bath had a crack in it half way up the side—a sign of Mary's struggle—making it difficult to keep the young ones washed.

Frankie's mates, using the place as a doss-house.

Daring to risk phoning up her estranged Granny June in East Belfast anonymously: "Is Mary there?"

"No, who is this?"

Click.

The R.U.C. left the McCandless children to their own resources—having arrested Frankie for riotous behaviour they came round to the flat. This was four days after Christmas. "Your parents need to come down to the station to sign the release forms."

Natalie told them: "My Daddy's dead and my Mum has not been seen nor heard of for weeks."

They told her: "You'll need to come with us then and sort it out."

No further questions were asked—it was obviously too much hassle.

A huge row with Frankie on what to do. Natalie wants to go to the civil rights people at N.I.C.R.A. and tell them what happened. "Whose side are you on?" Frankie leaves the house in protest and goes and lives with Granny Brigid.

Her Majesty's Social Services let the McCandless children down. Where were the Social Services for the month and a half Natalie waited for her mother to come back? And the truancy officers—did the school fail to notice that there wasn't a McCandless in the Nativity play?

You might well ask where were their Donard Flats neighbours?

You might indeed pour scorn on the vigilance of local priest?

None of the parties to the conflict, the war in Ulster, helped the McCandless children. Eventually they were taken into care, the family was split up and became estranged and exchanged hate for love.

34

Donal watched, shovel in hand, as two oyster catchers skimmed low over the stilled twilit waters of Carlingford Lough, their high-pitched cries haunting.

And further out to sea, the Irish Sea, a sea mist blocked sight of the North, where Greencastle should be, and the Mourne Mountains roll down to the sea.

This isolated spot was Churchtown Strand.

It had been selected as the final resting place of Mary McCandless by Joe's old Dundalk contact, your man Fergus Rafferty: "Believe me, no one will ever find her there!"

These last two days, he and Dec' (Jim's presence had not been required) had merely been obeying the black-bearded-if-balding Rafferty's barked orders. *The sheer amount of shite he'd had to go through because of the bitch's... (Don't speak ill of the dead—his Ma's voice)...because of the accident.* Their circuitous route south to Louth—nerve-jangling nail-biting at times—had been carefully and successfully plotted through the back roads of Armagh, Tyrone, Cavan, Monaghan, and Meath, to avoid detection by the Brit and Irish security forces.

There was a strange sound to this beach: a noise that can only be described as a 'swishing'—

Was it from the face-freezing on-shore breeze moving in waves through the sharp rushes on the dune-slacks all around?

Or was the flux of the sea on the shore?

Or, the particles of sand shifting beneath his feet, the dunes being driven inexorably inland by tide and wind, the whole place a movement in itself?

He didn't know.

He didn't know... Truth was, he'd been wracked by doubts, self-questionings, wondering *was this the right thing to do?* as the burial party had silently driven the final stretch; north up the Cooley Peninsula from Greenore in an old Escort that belonged to Rafferty's cousin. *What about her family?* He kept thinking. *Those kids we took her from, that boy back in the bar who for a second there seemed to have recognised me, will never know where she is...*

Now, standing over the grave, this rabbit scrape in this bare bunker of sand at the base of the dunes, barely three feet deep, he knew it was not right, Brit-lover, informer, or not...

He wanted to do something to make it right. But there was nothing more he could do than his duty. The marker had been called in, automatically. The Movement had moved. *What is done is done, and cannot be undone.*

The surface sand, dry and fly-away, had been easy to shift aside. The damp sand beneath, harder, more granite-grainy, but he had done most of the digging, and the others had allowed him, because they obviously felt he was mostly to blame.

A grunting and groaning Rafferty and Dec' lifted her out of the car boot in an old red blanket—

"Jesus, she's beginning to ming a bit so she is," Dec' said.

Rafferty and Dec' shuffled their way over the small rivulet, ten yards further to the hole, and one, two, flopped her down at the edge.

He rammed the shovel down into the mound of sand he'd made, a mini-avalanche slid into the pit.

They unfurled her out of the makeshift shroud, her body

148

stiffened and blued by death in the blood-stained rose-patterned dress; and in the process, he saw on her clawed-up hand that she was still wearing her rings.

"Wait a mo'," he said and went over to her. He knelt down beside her, took her hand and slid the three of them off—it was as if she didn't want to let go—her fingers curled tight.

"Good idea," said Rafferty, "Less to identify her—if they ever find her."

He put the rings in his pocket.

Rafferty toe-rolled her into the hole. "Start shovelling. And hurry up will you. It'd freeze your bollocks off out here."

The shovel—he got to his feet, walked over the shovel. Took hold of the handle. *That's it, bury the guilt with her—what guilt, it was an accident?* Digging—the first hiss of sand went in over her face.

"Jesus," said Rafferty, fumbling in his jacket pocket, bring-ing out a paper packet, "I almost forgot the quick-lime."

Bending, pouring, shaking the whiteness in, a fine dust, covering the whole body. This alkaline agent, a farm stores product, would chemically react with the increasing acidity of the body in breakdown, significantly hastening the process of decomposition.

Rafferty put the packet back into his pocket. "There, we're done."

The shovel scooped and into the hole. And another scoop. And another. And another. Quick as you like. *It's not your fault.* Until she was gone.

*

Geneva Convention I, for the amelioration of the condition of the Wounded and Sick in the Armed Forces in the Field. Article 17: Parties to the conflict shall ensure that burial or cremation of the dead, carried out individually as far as circumstances permit, is preceded by a careful examination, if possible a medical examination, of the bodies, with a view to confirming death, establishing identity and enabling a report to be made... They shall further ensure that the dead are honourably interred, if possible according to the rites of the religion to which they belonged, that their graves are respected...properly maintained and marked properly so that they may always be found... As soon as circumstances permit, and at the latest at the end of hostilities... (Grave Registration) *Services shall exchange...lists showing the exact location of the graves, together with the particulars of the dead interred therein.*

Mary's Final Resting Place

Shona Foyle, The Irish Telegraph,

(1st November 2004)

Mary McCandless, the mother of five who was abducted and killed by the IRA 32 years ago, was finally laid to rest in Lisburn cemetery today, in the same plot as her husband, Harold McCandless, who died in 1972.

The funeral follows a ten week long forensic analysis of her remains which were discovered by accident in a shallow grave on Churchtown Strand last July by a man walking his dog.

DNA tests on the skeletal remains were carried out in England and compared to genetic samples taken from her children. The results confirmed that this was indeed the body of the missing woman but the extensive post-mortem examination could not conclusively state the cause of death. Mrs McCandless had sustained blunt trauma injuries to her body but the exact cause of death is recorded by the coroner as unknown.

The IRA has admitted responsibility for her death, claiming she had been an informer—an allegation her family continues to vigorously deny. Her son, Frank McCandless, spoke out after the funeral service: 'After thirty years of Hell my mother is resting at peace. I had to forgive her killers a long time ago for my own sake. What I won't forget is how they dirtied her name all these years with their lies. She was not an informer. She helped a wounded soldier. That was why they did what they did, God help them.'

Bishop Joseph McCarthy told mourners at the funeral— including 100 members of the extended McCandless family, as well as members of the Families of the Disappeared—that her death had not only devastated the lives of her children and their children but that the disappearance of her body dehumanised her killers and had 'plumbed the depths of depravity'.

Natalie Kelly, who fought so hard to keep her mother's memory and those of the other so-called 'Disappeared' alive in the media said: 'Finally, I have a grave to visit, and I hope that I can find some closure. This is what I wished for through all those dark days and long nights.'

Simon Kerr was born in Belfast in 1971. He has written two other novels: *The Rainbow Singer* (2001) and *As Seen on TV* (2005).

White Sand is a homage to Joyce Carol Oates' political novel, *Black Water*. It is dedicated to all the Disappeared of Northern Ireland. The author owes a debt of gratitude to Jean McConville's daughter, Helen, and her husband, Seamus McKendry, author of *Disappeared: the Search for Jean McConville*, for their help in researching what happened to Jean and her family.

Also by the same author:

The Rainbow Singer

Wil is a teenage Heavy Metal fan who lives with his family in Belfast. He is sent with nine other Protestants, plus ten Catholic youngsters, to Milwaukee USA as part of a month-long peace initiative. The organisers of 'Project Ulster' are full of optimism, but the Project goes wrong from the start. Wil is not simply the angst-ridden, fourteen-year-old he appears to be. He lives a secret life as a Loyalist terrorist, and peace is the last thing on his mind.

That is, until he meets Teresa, a bewitching Catholic girl who makes him believe that the American Dream, where everyone can live together, might be possible. But when Teresa breaks Wil's heart, old grievances resurface. Egged on by Derry, his host family's son, Wil soon resorts to his old ways and events spiral out of control.

As Seen on TV

(under the pen-name of Chris Kerr)
Kirk Rush is a struggling English screenwriter who is obsessed by the action TV shows of the 1980s. Now he's finally been offered his dream job of writing The A-Team movie - provided he can set it in the Gulf War and make Face bisexual. But Kirk's attempts to knuckle down to his script are thwarted by the news that his younger sister Denise has taken herself off dialysis in Miami and is planning to commit assisted suicide with the help of the notorious Dr Death and his 'Sisters of Mercy'. It will take all of his powers of imagination, not to mention the assistance of KITTSCH (his Knight Rider car-cum-conscience) to help him on his heroic quest to save her.

'Very funny, and perfect for any TV or film fan'
MATT THORNE